NICOLE WILLIAMS

ISBN-13: 978-1514622896
ISBN-10: 1514622890

Cover Design by Sarah Hansen of Okay Creations
Editing by Cassie Cox
Formatting by JT Formatting

PROLOGUE

SHE WAS MY heart. She was my soul. She was everything that resided in between.

I guessed that was just another way of saying she was my everything. That was what my mind kept circling back to ever since we'd scheduled the surgery. It was still a month out. I knew it was considered fairly low risk compared to other kinds of heart surgery, but when a doctor detailed what was involved—opening up my wife's chest, digging around inside to find that vital, pumping organ, moving on to repair what's wrong before closing her back up and sewing her shut—nothing about that sounded low risk. Low risk was stitching up a gash or setting a broken arm, not open heart surgery.

I'd struggled with nightmares for most of my life, but they'd always been the same. After the word "surgery" spilled out of the doctor's mouth though, I started having a different kind of nightmare. One still having to do with pain and blood and loss, but I wasn't starring in my night terrors any longer. It was her. Rowen.

Chained to an operating table instead of a rusty water pipe, her screams filled my head instead of my own. I could see her blood staining my hands when I lifted them in front of my face. Her life slowly drained out of her, seeming to puddle at my feet, while I stood there, frozen in time or in shock, unable to hold on to her as she slipped away.

It was a nightmare I'd become far too acquainted with, and one that woke me up too many times, the sheets tangled around me and sweat dripping down my body. The images always took too many moments to clear from my head. I didn't want to wake her, but sometimes I couldn't help it. If she didn't jerk awake from my screams or from my body flying up in bed—if by some miracle she managed to stay in her peaceful place—I found myself gently pressing my hand to her back, waiting to detect the faint beat. Sometimes it would take a moment for me to feel it, and in that panicked moment, I heard my own heartbeat thrumming in my ears, seeming to fill the entire room.

Every time, I've felt her heart's beat. Sometimes it takes me longer than other times to find it, but to date, I've always been able to make out that steady, confident beat fluttering inside her. Sometimes all I needed to feel was a few beats before it lulled me back to sleep. Other times, I'd see the light from the sunrise filter through the window before I could pry my hand away from her back to crawl into the shower and get started with the day.

The more a person thought about a heart and how it just kept going—beat after beat, hour after hour, decade after decade—the more of a miracle it became. The more of a mystery it seemed to be. This thing that pumped blood through our body, keeping it alive—it never stopped, never faltered, could endure extreme amounts of stress and abuse . . .

Right up until it gave out.

That was what I'd been thinking about lately. A heart. More specifically, Rowen's heart. It was fine and healthy and strong until it wasn't. That was the way it was for all of us, I fully understood that, but it took on a different meaning when someone close to you was told their heart wasn't right. The words the doctor said kept replaying in my head, over and over. Words like ventricles and narrowing and operating and risks of stress. Words that were, on their own, unthreatening, but when tied to the woman I loved, they took on material form. Almost as if surgery shifted into the shape of a gun and all the other words materialized into bullets, one after another being loaded into that gun before it dropped to the temple of the person I cared about most in the world.

I'd heard it said that words were only words, but that wasn't true. At least not all of the time. Words had power. Words had more power than a man's fists or a woman's stare. They had a hundred times more power than people gave them credit for, and that was what a portion of their power was derived from—humanity's aversion to ascribing power to those seemingly innocent things we called words.

I knew better though now. I knew just how much power words had after enduring countless hours in waiting rooms, patient rooms, and doctors' offices over the past couple of months. I knew words might not be able to take Rowen away from me, but they were responsible for paving the path.

"Words don't have power," people still tried to tell me. Then why hadn't I gotten a good night's sleep since the day I rushed Rowen to urgent care after she passed out in the middle of the track we were running on? Why hadn't I had a half a day of peace since the tests they ran that day were explained to us?

If words didn't have power, why had I been holding my breath for her heart to give out at any second?

The answer was simple, so I didn't know why everyone seemed to refuse to accept it. Words were the single most powerful thing on the planet. I wouldn't forget that. Especially when a doctor told me we were just going to discuss the options and go over the risks associated with those options. I'd make sure to cut him off when he started listing what could happen before, during, or after surgery when a person had a heart defect like Rowen's. I'd make sure to lift a hand to silence him when he, in so many words, said my wife had a bad heart.

How could that be? How was it even humanly possible that this person who was the very definition of love and heart and soul to me could have a bad heart? How was that for the most cruel, morbid form of irony?

Rowen had a bad heart.

That was a load of bullshit.

Rowen had the truest, most pure, good heart I'd ever known. That was what I tried to comfort myself with when I felt the stirrings of a panic attack creeping up from my stomach. I knew the heart I saw in Rowen and the heart the cardiologist saw in her were wholly different things, but that didn't stop me from trying to grasp onto whatever strand of hope I found dangling above my head.

I didn't know how long I'd been sitting behind the wheel in Old Bessie, staring through the windshield and seeing nothing but my fears seeming to take real shapes and forms before my eyes. I saw tragedy blooming in the flowers lining the walkway to our new condo. I saw death shoving through the soil, growing into the grass edging the sidewalk. I saw a life void of love and color and laughter in the wisp of clouds dotting the blue Seattle sky. I saw death where there was life. I saw darkness where there was light. I saw pain and heartache and tragedy on a beautiful summer day . . . and I wanted it to go away. I wanted to believe the best and hold on to so much hope I was drowning in it, but even all my supposed optimism was struggling to see the good in this. From a husband's standpoint, there was no good in finding out my wife had a heart condition that required surgery sooner rather than later. No good side at all.

I shifted in my seat and blinked a few times in an attempt to clear the images from my head. They were only flowers. Only grass. Only clouds. It didn't work, so I turned my attention to the cab and took a few deep breaths. Everything would be fine. Rowen would be fine. She'd have the surgery, recover without a glitch, and we could go on with life as if this had never happened.

Instead of reassuring myself by focusing on the familiarity of Old Bessie's cab, I saw Rowen sitting beside me, dangling her arm out of the window. That faded, and I found the seat empty again, but the image was still seared in my brain. I wondered if that side of the truck would one day go unoccupied, the spot where she sat never to warm again, the pictures she liked to scroll into the windows after spending a night steaming them up having been drawn for the last time. Rowen saw the world as her canvas, and she never wasted an opportunity to leave her mark, even if it was just on a plate of steamed up glass.

I shook my head, realizing it was hopeless. It didn't matter where I looked or where I tried to seek solace. Even

Old Bessie couldn't provide a measure of comfort anymore. The threat of losing her was too real. I couldn't find comfort when there was none to begin with.

Then something caught my attention from the corner of my eye. In an instant, the weight pressing on my chest lifted and I could breathe fully again. In the span of one breath, I had a flash that everything would be okay. How could it not be? To watch her casually pedaling down the sidewalk, her face angled toward the sky as the corners of her mouth pulled up . . . how could anything happen to her? How could anything happen to one of the earth's greatest creations? It couldn't. It wouldn't be possible.

She lived in shades of black and gray—sometimes a dark purple will slip in in the form of shoelaces or a headband—but she painted the entire world with color. She painted *my* entire world with color. It was as if before her, I was going through life in black and white, not realizing there was this whole other world filled with texture and color and unspeakable beauty.

She painted the whole world for me, and if she was taken away from me, the color would leave with her. My world would go back to black and white, except this time, I'd know the difference. I'd know there was something so much better, and I'd want it back. I'd want it back, but if she were gone, I could never have it back. I could never have her back.

The weight heaved back down on my chest, spilling the oxygen from my lungs.

She still rode that same bike I used to cringe at when she first moved here, but I'd added so many bells and whistles and baskets to it that we'd managed to strike a somewhat happy medium. When we first found out about

Rowen's heart, I said the bike had to go and that we finally had to break down and buy a second car. Her tale of that story is that I flat-out ordered her, but I preferred the term "begged without abate." Of course the harder I shoved my heels into the ground, the more she did, and really, she's much better at heel digging than I am. She said it was because she'd had more practice, but I was inclined to believe it had more to do with my inability to say more than a string of a few nos to her before giving in, giving up, or letting go. In short, she won twice as many points of contention as I did.

She claimed she won the bike battles—*all* of them—but I preferred to see it as reaching a mutually satisfactory conclusion. Kind of. The bike remained her main mode of transportation because she agreed to wear a heart rate monitor and promised to keep her heart rate below sixty percent of her max. She said that was overkill and didn't want to strap on some giant watch that read her pulse everywhere she went, but the doctor admitted my idea wasn't a bad one, so with the help of what Rowen had dubbed her doctor's and my "Dark Side," she gave in and strapped on the giant, ugly watch before she went anywhere on her bike.

She said it wasn't only a fashion faux-pas but a waste of money to boot, because she'd been riding her bike for years and hadn't had any problems with it straining her heart. She'd likely been born with her condition and had managed just fine until she'd decided to give running a try. Two decades she'd been living with this, and it took trying to run wind sprints, followed by passing out, for a doctor to diagnose her.

The bike slowed as she neared our condo. I found

myself glancing at her wrist to make sure she had it on. She did. It wasn't so ugly to me. Yeah, it was big enough that it seemed to take up a quarter of her forearm, but that device would keep her from straining her heart. It would alert her if she was pushing herself too hard. It helped keep her alive. That made it worth every single hour of overtime I'd worked last month to pay for it.

When she reached the bottom of the apartment stairs and chained her bike to the rail, I found my motivation to pry myself from the confines of Old Bessie. When I shoved the door, it whined open. It didn't wail as it had before Rowen got it all cherried out for me a couple of years ago, but it was an old truck. It deserved to creak and whine and moan.

Rowen must have heard the telltale sound because her head whipped in my direction, her smile moving higher when she saw me weaving through the condo's parking lot toward her. "Hey, cowboy! I didn't think I'd see you for another few hours. They've been keeping you so busy I've almost forgotten what that fine ass of yours looks like."

Of course that was the moment our neighbors in the condo below us opened their front door. Their brows first lifted at us before lifting a degree higher when they looked at each other.

Noticing them and their pronounced eyebrows, Rowen tilted her head at me, a smirk in place. "I mean your aesthetically pleasing backside." She winked at me as I crossed the last few steps toward her.

Our neighbors kept going as if they hadn't noticed us, but I was figuring out that that was the big city way. People were stacked on top of each other, but they all pretended they didn't notice the person two feet in front of them.

Although, based on Rowen's assumptions, our neighbors knew everything about us and were probably keeping a diary of complaints for the manager, including how long our showers were; when, how long, and how loud we made love; and how often we walked down the hallway in the middle of the night. She called them the Nosey Newburgs, but they didn't seem so bad. Or so different from the rest of the people I'd met in Seattle.

"Hi yourself, beautiful." I shot a wave at the Newburgs, but if it was acknowledged, it didn't get returned.

Rowen crossed her arms as I leapt onto the sidewalk. "I know you didn't just call me beautiful. I *know* you didn't just stoop to some lame, generic identifier meant to objectify and go against pretty much everything I stand for. Right?"

Instead of answering her, I hitched an arm around her waist and pulled her close. I knew better than to jump into this kind of discussion with her, mainly because she always won.

"Call me edgy, call me spunky. Rough around the edges even. Anything but pretty or sweet or beautiful." She wrinkled up her nose and attempted to shiver, but the closer I pulled her to me, the more fake the act became.

When she lifted an eyebrow, clearly waiting for my response to come in some form other than winding my arms around her, I shrugged. "Sorry. When I look at you, that's all I see. Beauty. I can't change what I see, and I wouldn't want to either. You're beautiful, whether you refuse to see it or not."

She tried to glare at me. She failed big time. She gave up with a sigh and rolled her eyes. "Fine. But you are the *only* one who can call me the b-word."

I gave her a squeeze then kissed her forehead before moving toward her bike to grab the shopping bags stuffed into the baskets I'd fastened to the bike. "You know, most girls mean a totally different word when they talk about a 'b-word.'"

"And the day I can be grouped in with 'most girls,' then maybe I'll bat my eyes and go all wobbly-kneed when someone calls me beautiful. In the meantime, use it sparingly." She nudged me as she shouldered up beside me, reaching for one of the bags.

"I've got it," I said, slipping the bag away from her.

"Please don't make me feel like an invalid. We've talked about this." Rowen glanced at the bags in my hands and waited.

"You just rode your bike lord knows how far and have to climb a steep set of stairs to our condo now. I think you've stressed your body enough without heaving twenty pounds of groceries up said stairs." I stepped back when she reached for one of the bags. I wasn't giving in. I wasn't. I gave in all the time, but this was important. Where her health and life was concerned, it was critically important.

She threw her arm in the direction of the stairs. "Why are you acting like trudging up a flight of stairs is like scaling K-2 in a pair of Keds?"

"Why are you acting like climbing them is like taking a nap under a tree in the summer?" I would have waved at the stairs too, but my hands were too full with the groceries.

"Because they're stairs. Twenty of them, the last time I counted. Hardly enough to get my heart rate up any more than if I *was* taking that nap under that tree." Her voice was level, calm almost.

Rowen was as used to getting into these kinds of squabbles as I was. We had plenty of them. Daily, sometimes hourly. I'd gotten used to it and had accepted that the reason we argued our point was because we cared. If I didn't care so much about her, it would be much easier to just give in and wave her up the stairs with bags of groceries about to tumble out of her arms. If she didn't care so much about me, it would be much easier for her to just let me turn into an anxious creature who had watched her every step since the words "heart condition" filtered through that doctor's office.

We argued because we cared. Seemed kind of backward, but not once I'd really given it some thought.

"Let me help. Please, Rowen. I'm here. Last time I checked, I'm pretty damn strong." I curled my arm so my bicep pressed through the material of my T-shirt. She tried not to notice, but her eyes lingered. "Not to mention I've got close to two decades of experience carrying groceries. I can get through this, but I need you to let me help where I can."

She pinched at my arm then glided her pinkie along the seams of the muscles winding down my bicep and forearm. Her lightest, most simple touch could still trickle through me and chase away the fears and hurts and worries I didn't even know I'd been carrying. She might have liked to consider herself rough around the edges, but she was the most gentle, soothing spirit I'd ever been around.

"Okay, I get you want to help. I get you *need* to help," she said, wrapping her fingers around my wrist. "But I've been thinking, and I'm confident I need to lay some additional ground rules."

"*Additional* ground rules?" I sighed; there'd been additions to the additions already. "What kind of additional ground rules?"

Her hand went to her hip as the other, still wound around my wrist, tightened. "Ground rules that include you not trying to strap my watch on in the middle of us making love so you can make sure my heart rate isn't nearing the danger zone."

I shifted the groceries in my hands. "That wasn't what happened . . ."

"No, because I grabbed the thing and threw it across the room before your fingers could curl around it." She moved closer, an evil smile twisting into place. "Then I did that one thing that makes your forget your name, let alone some stupid watch reading my heart rate."

I felt a stupid smile creep into place as I remembered last night. "That's a ground rule I can accept, but I might need a repeat just to make sure I can resist the temptation. Practice makes perfect, right?"

Rowen's gaze lowered to the bags, the skin between her eyebrows just barely creasing. "You've had no shortage of practice, that's for sure."

When she bit her lip, that's when the first alert in my mind went off.

"What's going on?" I asked, lowering my head so I could look into her eyes. She was far better than I was at hiding her emotions, but if I could get a good solid look in those eyes of hers, I could usually catch a hint at what was wrong. If had only taken me a few years to start to figure it out . . .

"Jesse," she said, the slightest of warnings in her tone.

"Rowen." I gave it right back to her, but she was already heading up the stairs.

"If we keep bickering out here, the yogurt's going to go bad," she called back at me, pulling her keys out of her purse.

"The threat of yogurt going bad isn't going to make me drop this."

"I don't know what you're talking about."

"Delay, if you will," I said, bounding up the stairs after her, "but I'm only giving you a few minutes. Five max."

She had the key in the lock and was shoving the door open when I leapt up the last couple of stairs. "Good thing I'm a pro at distracting you and rendering your brain into mush. Your intentions become putty in my hands when I turn on my feminine prowess and beguile you with my wanton passion."

I gave her a peculiar look. "You've been reading those books Lily sent you, haven't you? The ones with the swoopy fonts, and oiled up men, and women looking ravished in their arms?"

"The bodice-rippers?" She shut the door and followed me into the kitchen, which wasn't far since our condo was about a coat closet larger than my attic bedroom at Willow Springs. "No, I could barely stomach the first page of the first one I picked up. What she sees in them, I don't know, but I guess romance is kind of like everything else—everyone has a different cup of tea."

"And what's your cup of tea?" I dropped the bags onto the kitchen counter and turned to face her.

"You." She pinched the brim of my hat and tugged it lower on my forehead. "You're my cup of tea."

A grin worked into place on my face. When she saw

it, she slid the bill of my hat down farther so it covered my eyes.

"That might be the sweetest thing you've ever said to me," I said as I readjusted my hat back into place. Then I noticed the look on her face and recognized my poor choice of words. "I mean . . . that was the most edgy, spunky, rough-around-the-edges thing you've ever said to me."

She chuckled as she shook her head. "That's two, Walker. One more, and you're out."

"Out of what?"

As she started sorting through the grocery bags, I slid up beside her to help. She seemed to be looking for something in them more than actually being concerned with putting the food away though.

"Out of luck for getting laid tonight," she said, pillaging through the next bag.

"Ouch. My lips are sealed with that threat on the table. Consider me mute from now until we tumble into bed just in case I make another slip."

"Such a man," she mumbled, tearing through the second bag.

"Hey, let me help you before that vein in your forehead ruptures."

Her face was screwed tight with concentration. I reached into the third bag, which she hadn't gotten to yet. The first thing my fingers curled around, I pulled out of the bag. I had to lift it up in front of my face and read what was written on the box three times before it processed.

Beside me, a curse slipped past Rowen's lips. "You found it. Thanks."

My eyes narrowed as I studied the rectangular box for

a few more seconds, as if I was expecting the words to read something different the next time. "What's this for?"

Rowen's shoulders fell as she shoved the grocery bags farther down the counter like they'd betrayed her. "I'm doing this new art show with fertility as the theme. Totally cutting edge. Avant-garde all the way. I thought using pregnancy tests as a medium would score me some creativity points in the ironic department."

When she reached for the box, I lifted it out of her reach. My forehead couldn't have creased any deeper.

"They're for me, crazy," she said, jumping to try to snag the box away from me. "What do you think they're for?"

I swallowed so hard I felt my Adam's apple drop a foot before bobbing back into place. "Like, just to have for one day in the future, right? A just in case precaution? Not to use, as in, right now? Right?" How many rights could I fit in one breath?

She let out a long sigh then, moving so quickly she caught me off guard, her fingers wrapped around the box and snatched it out of my grasp. She was halfway down the hall before I'd realized what had happened.

"Rowen? What's going on? Not a fan of being left in the dark. Especially when my wife shows up with a box of pregnancy tests when she absolutely, positively, most certainly could *not* be pregnant."

Before I could catch up to her, she disappeared into the bathroom and sealed the door. When I tried to open it, I found she'd locked it. I could already feel my heart in the back of my throat, but then I tasted it—the metallic, bitter taste of panic filling my mouth.

"Yeah, that's why I was hoping to beat you home,"

she hollered. "So you wouldn't need to go through any undue stress if this turns out to be nothing."

"If *what* turns out to be nothing?" I called back, hovering on the other side of the door. The last minute had happened so quickly, I couldn't catch up to what was happening. What that box meant. What her disappearing behind the bathroom door with it meant. What her wanting to beat me home meant.

"If I turn out to be pregnant." Her voice wasn't quite so loud now, but it hit me as if she'd just dropped a grenade in front of me.

I had to take a couple of breaths before I could work up any sort of reply. "But we're on, like, every form of birth control known to mankind."

"Every kind but one."

I heard what sounded like the box being ripped open, but I couldn't be sure because everything from the time she'd said the word pregnant in reference to herself was a blur of total and utter confusion.

"I don't understand . . ." I said to her reply and everything that had happened in the last two and a half minutes.

"Abstinence."

My face screwed together. "That's barbaric."

"Well, you're the one who brought up the birth control subject."

I didn't understand how she could sound so calm—so in control of her emotions. How could she go on acting and talking to me as if this was any old day, any old conversation, while she was taking a test to determine whether she was or wasn't pregnant? Didn't she understand what it meant if she was? Hadn't she been sitting next to me while the doctor cautioned us to use every contraceptive measure possible until after the surgery? Hadn't the ramifications and dangers computed in her head the way they had in mine? How could she talk to me as though her heart wasn't about to burst out of her chest or her knees weren't about to give out, like mine felt close to doing?

"Rowen?" I knocked on the door and tried the door handle again. I didn't like being on this side of the door when she was on the other side, having her future revealed to her alone. "Let me in. Please?"

On the other side, there was silence.

"Rowen?" My knocks turned to pounds as I imagined the worst—her passed out on the tile from taxing her heart from the bike ride or the stairs or the shock of finding out . . . "Rowen! Please. Open the door."

Another moment of silence. All I could hear was my heart beating in my ears before the door in front of me opened.

She stuck out her head, and even though she was biting at her lip like crazy, she lifted her eyes to mine. "Do you want the good news or the bad news first?" She didn't seem to blink as she watched me. "The good news, right?"

"Usually, yeah," I answered, focusing on her because she was the only thing in the room that wasn't spinning. "But let's switch it up today. Give me the bad news first."

Her teeth sank deeper into her lip. "We're going to need to buy a new car."

I waited for her to add something. When it was clear she was waiting for me to say something else, I cleared my throat. "That's not bad news. I've been trying to get you a mode of transportation that has four wheels instead of two wheels for years. What kind are you thinking?"

Her head tilted as she gave me a curious look. I knew

that look. It meant I wasn't getting it.

"I don't know," she said. "I think a mini-van's the no-brainer option, but maybe we could manage with a roomy sedan."

"A mini-van? I thought I'd see you in a pair of chaps before I'd see you in a mini-van."

Another look from her, this one even more pronounced. I *really* wasn't getting it.

"Along with that mini-van, we'll need to grab a car seat, and one of those mirrors so the driver can see into the backseat, and a case or five of diapers, and probably those stick figure decals people display on their back windows because . . ." She lifted her hand. In it was clutched a white plastic stick with one end showing two pink lines. "Because baby makes three."

The air left my lungs in one quick rush . . . then what she said started to sink in. Two pink lines. Baby makes three. Car seats. Diapers. Was she saying? Was Rowen . . .?

"Are you pregnant?" My voice didn't sound like my own. It sounded like a stranger's.

She lifted another test stick into the air. Two pink lines on that one too. "Either I'm pregnant, or this company has got some serious quality control issues."

This time it didn't just feel as if the air had been robbed from my lungs—it felt as if they'd collapsed in on themselves.

"What's the good news?" I asked, curling my fingers into her side. It was like she was already slipping away, and I would hold on for as long and as hard as I could.

I couldn't be sure, because it flashed across her face so quickly, but it looked as if pain flooded her eyes and lined her face. "The good news is that I'm pregnant, Jesse Walker. With *our* child. With your future son or daughter. Our baby is growing inside me right this very moment . . . which reminds me, I need to eat lunch." She smiled, waiting for me to join her. When my face stayed a mask of shock and what I guessed was dismay, her smile disappeared. "You're not taking the good news like I thought you would."

So much coming at me. Hit after hit after hit. As soon as I'd managed to regain my balance, the next assault came at me, reeling me back over. I was so turned upside down, I didn't know if I was flat on my feet or on my back.

"This isn't good news, Rowen. Why are you expecting me to take this like it's good news?" Every few words, I had to take a breath, but it didn't seem to help. My lungs felt collapsed and shriveled and useless.

She blinked. "How is our baby *not* good news? How can you imply that me being pregnant with our baby is anything *but* good news?"

When she blinked again, a tear slipped out of the corner of her eye. I'd grown so accustomed to Rowen's seeming inability to cry, I'd almost convinced myself that I'd imagined it until another tear slipped out of the corner of the same eye. She was crying, or she'd shed two tears, because of me. Because of what I'd said and how I was reacting to the news. It was enough to break through my shell of shock.

Scrubbing at my face, I exhaled. "You're asking me to celebrate something that might very well kill you. How can you expect me to look at this as good news?"

Her face broke for a moment, then the resolve I was

used to seeing carved in her expression took hold. Opening the door all of the way, she grabbed my hand and lowered it to her stomach. She slid it under her shirt and splayed my fingers against her skin, pressing it so firmly against her that I could feel her heartbeat thrumming against my palm from her belly button.

"This isn't about me right now, Jesse. This is about the living thing inside of me the two of us created."

My hand warmed from her skin. My heart started to slow to match her steady, rhythmic beat.

"I know neither one of us would have chosen to have a baby right now, with everything going on with me and my troublemaker of a heart, but we don't always get to choose the hand we're dealt. All we can control is how we play that hand—from a place of fear or a place of hope." Her fingers curled through mine, holding on to me as if she also felt the slipping away sensation and was doing everything to hang on. "I don't know why I'm the one siding with hope and you seem to be siding with the other when our whole lives we've done the opposite, but I could really use you on my side with this. I could really, really use your support." She moved closer, fitting her body into mine before wrapping an arm around me. Our hands stayed tied together and pressed against her stomach. "I'm scared too, you know? This is all coming at me as fast as it's coming at you. I'm not refusing to admit this is dangerous and less than ideal and going to be a terrifying journey, but I'm choosing to let the good overshadow the bad. I won't let what might happen rob me of everything wonderful that can and will happen as a result of this."

I found myself shaking my head when I knew I should have been nodding. She was saying everything that made sense and everything I'd say to her if things were different, but I couldn't. Not with her life on the line. "You could die. Having this baby could kill you."

She looked at me with big searching eyes. "I won't let the fear of dying take away the absolute wonder and joy of this tiny little life. I won't let death take away the excitement of life." Her hand around me pulled me closer. "Can you do that with me? *Will* you do this with me?"

In one part of my head, I knew we were talking about Rowen and I having a baby. I knew that for most married, loving couples, this was the kind of news that inspired jumping around rooms and screaming before dialing phone numbers and screaming in family members' ears. I knew that if Rowen was healthy and didn't have a heart condition that could potentially kill her and I'd just found out about her being pregnant, I would have been so overwhelmed with amazement and joy that I would have been spinning Rowen around instead of clinging to her as though I was afraid someone was tugging her away from me. But I couldn't get past the crippling horror and panic of this change bringing my wife face to face with the very real threat of losing her life. I couldn't see past the great black tower of fear and dread to catch a glimpse of the light and peace on the other side.

All I could think about was Rowen . . . and the possibility of her one day not existing. The possibility of being unable to pull her into my arms whenever I wanted or wake up in the dead of night and let her rhythmic breathing lull me back to sleep. She was woven into every part of my life, down to the last thread, and I couldn't picture my life without her in it.

It felt like half a lifetime had passed before I could

say anything. "I'm scared."

Rowen lowered her head to my chest. My hand skimmed up her back and settled into the bend of her neck, holding her so close to my chest.

"I am too," she whispered into my shirt. "It's okay. Be scared with me. But don't forget to be happy too."

Happy? How could I be happy when I knew what this meant? Rowen. Her heart. It might not be able to handle the stresses of pregnancy. Rowen . . . was asking me to be happy with her. She was asking me to be happy with her *for* her. At the same time I knew that was impossible, I knew it was impossible not to give her what she needed.

Squeezing my eyes shut, I forced all remnants of worry and images of death aside. She was waiting for my response, so I nodded. I would *try* to be happy too. No guarantees, but I'd try.

"You're going to be a dad." Her words were muffled against my chest, but I heard the smile in her voice. I felt her smile in the air.

I wanted to return the sentiment. *You're going to be a mom.* But the first word stuck in my throat, making it impossible for the rest to follow. Instead, I somehow managed to pull her closer, trying to silence the question cycling through my head. *Will that baby ever get a chance to know its mom?*

CHAPTER one

Jesse

Three Months Later

I'D BEEN STARING at her for so long, my eyes felt as if they were about to start watering. *Blink, Jesse*, I had to say to myself. It was all kinds of ridiculous that I had to remind myself to blink, but I'd found things that used to come instinctually weren't so natural anymore and things that hadn't come naturally were now hard-wired into my instincts.

Things like sleeping, reaching for a bottle of water when my throat had turned into a cylinder of sandpaper, putting on a jacket when it was cold, taking *off* a layer when it was hot, reaching for something to eat when my stomach was about to stage a revolt, changing the position I was sitting in when my leg fell asleep . . . kind of like it was at that very moment. Oh, and of course, blinking, because why would that come naturally?

Shifting my position on the overstuffed chair that had been dragged into the middle of the condo, I shook my so-numb-it-was-bordering-on-painful leg and tried not to let it reflect in my expression.

"If I wanted you to move, I'd be over there, crawling into your lap and making you move." Rowen stuck her head out from behind the giant canvas propped up on an easel, brow raised and brush pointed my way. "Now, for the five hundredth time, hold still please."

"Sorry," I mouthed, careful to move as few facial muscles as possible.

Keeping her warning look aimed my way for a moment more, she relented with a wink before disappearing behind the canvas again. Instantly, my stare dropped to the wood floor, where I could see her feet and up to her knees before the bottom of the canvas hid the rest of her from view.

I'd developed a nifty new tick since Rowen had flashed two pink lines in my face a few months earlier: the inability to not keep her in my sights when we were together. It didn't matter if we were two feet apart or if she was doing nothing more ambitious than snoozing on the sofa—if she was in view, she was in *my* view at all times. I didn't know where it had come from or how I'd let it develop to the extreme it had without catching it first, but my best guess was that my mind had somehow rationalized that if I could see her, then she couldn't disappear. If I was watching her, nothing could tear her away from me. If I kept her in my sights, nothing would happen to her.

It wasn't logical or rational or something I could explain without feeling like I'd just escaped from a straitjacket, but it wasn't exactly like love fell into any of those categories either. So I accepted it. I accepted what I felt and how it had manifested in the form of instinct and habit.

Old programmed responses became replaced with

new ones. The new ones consisted of resting my hand flat against her back every night I crawled in beside her and concentrating on the beat thrumming against her bone and muscle and skin. The sun rose more often with my eyes still open, hand still in place, than ones where my body had found the refuge of sleep.

Phone calls had become another fun experiment in torture. If my phone rang when I wasn't with Rowen, my world would blur and my heart would stop, sure the caller was waiting to reveal to me that my wife's heart had done just that. Stopped. Given out. Given up.

Those examples just barely scraped the surface of what sorts of new habits I'd developed as a result of Rowen's pregnancy, but God only knew how many more would crop up in the last few months leading up to the delivery.

"This is like *the* best dinner ever." From behind the canvas, Rowen's arm popped out. Her hand curled around the fork propped on the plate on the stool, holding a stack of pancakes. She cut a wedge off from the quickly diminishing tower, stabbed all six layers, and her arm, hand, and fork disappeared behind the canvas. "You can cook for me anytime you want. You know, for future reference," she said through a mouthful of pancake.

I wasn't supposed to move, but a smile twitched at the corners of my mouth. Thankfully, she hadn't popped her head back out to notice. "That's because it's not dinner. It's dessert."

Her hand reappeared to drop the fork back on the plate before slipping behind the canvas. The smile kept tugging at the corners of my mouth when I noticed the smears of paint streaked along her hands and forearms.

Rowen always told me you could tell how good a piece of art would turn out based on how messy you got creating it. From the looks of just her left arm and hand, she was creating a masterpiece. Monet, watch your back—Rowen Sterling-Walker's coming to get you.

"It's love on a plate. That's what it is." She popped up onto her tiptoes, giving her just enough clearance to peer over the top of the canvas at me.

Since I'd been laser-focused on her legs and feet, I was able to stifle my smile before I earned my five-hundredth-and-one warning. Her head tilted a bit, her eyes narrowing in a concentrated kind of way, before disappearing again. I'd gotten used to getting flashes of Rowen, pieces of her, bits at a time, every Friday night for the past couple of months. Well, this was Thursday night, but Friday was our typical night for me to cook her dinner before she held me prisoner in the overstuffed chair until an hour or two after midnight. Tomorrow night, though, we'd be rolling into Willow Springs to kick off our trial summer, so Rowen had pretty much demanded that we move up our date night by twenty-four hours. She'd been working on whatever the painting was—she wouldn't let me see yet—since we'd found out she was pregnant, and she said she was getting close to finishing.

"Will you make this for me next Friday night too?" she asked, her voice muffled, which meant she had the handle of a paintbrush in her teeth. "Pancakes just taste better at Willow Springs."

"Yeah, but those aren't *just* pancakes. Those are chocolate chips pancakes with peanut butter layered in between."

I hadn't been hungry, but Rowen had refused to dig

into her stack until I did. She'd started noticing I wasn't eating, drinking, or sleeping during the first couple of weeks after we'd learned of her pregnancy. At first, she hadn't said too much, probably assuming it was a phase that would pass. When she observed it only seemed to get worse with time, she started to intervene in the way only Rowen was capable. So I'd shoveled down a plateful of pancakes I hadn't been hungry for so she would eat her own, and I was pleasantly surprised to discover chocolate chip pancakes smeared in peanut butter didn't taste just barely palatable but actually pretty damn good.

"Peanut butter, yum." Rowen sighed like she sighed my name when I slipped a sheet of her hair over her shoulder and kissed the base of her neck. "It's manna from the gods. Manna in creamy, roasted goodness conveniently packaged in a jar."

"I asked Mom to stock up on peanut butter, and she said she'd swiped every last jar of Skippy, Jiff, and generic brand peanut butter on the shelves at Murray's, so we should be good to go until next weekend at least."

"If your son grows any faster, it won't make it that long." The paintbrush wasn't in her mouth any longer. From the sounds of it, the brush had moved from her mouth to slashing frantic strokes across the canvas again.

Rowen thought we were having a boy. No, she was *convinced* we were having a boy. At the last appointment, we could have found out the gender of the baby if we wanted to, but we'd made the decision to wait to find out until the baby was born. Rowen liked a little mystery in her life and mentioned that the surprise would make the whole messy part of the Cesarean delivery a bit less so. Instead of just getting to see his or her face and count his or her toes, we'd be able to look forward to finding out if it was a his or a her. She said that would make the actual delivery less daunting and more fun . . . although I couldn't quite comprehend how anything could make getting one's stomach cut into "easier." I didn't have to comprehend it though because for her, it worked. It only endeared her that much more to me.

Which would only make it that much more difficult to lose her.

That was the main reason why I'd agreed to not find out the gender of the baby. Giving it a boy or girl designation usually led to a name, which led to outfitting a nursery, which led to a whole new world of expectations and anticipations I was all too okay with keeping the door closed on at that point. It felt too much like tempting bad luck to come hunt us down if we found out what the baby was, or gave it a name, or put together a nursery and prepared a diaper bag. We had enough bad luck stacked against us at it was—I didn't want to garner the attention of any more.

Rowen stuck her head out around the side of the canvas again, inspecting my face in only the way a person looking to know every scar, wrinkle, and imperfection so they could capture the bad with the good would. When she disappeared behind the painting again, I snuck in a yawn. Realizing the deaths of one's wife and unborn child were only about fifty times more likely had a way of keeping a man up at night.

"I'm used to hearing a subtle sigh or notice a tightening in your jaw or witness that the-end-is-near expression roll across your face whenever I mention my confidence on the gender." Rowen's voice trickled around the canvas and filled the small space of our condo. Her voice had always had a way of doing that—filling a room from one corner to the next. It wasn't like her voice was loud or harsh, like it sometimes got when we were in the heat of plenty of kinds of moments, but her voice, kind of like the rest of her, just had a way of filling the room. Not to mention my world. "Did you fall asleep over there?"

I gave my head a small shake to clear it before answering. "Not asleep. Not yet at least. Just trying to obey your every command and heed your every threat to not move a muscle. Last I checked, sighing, jaw tightening, and the-end-is-near looks required moving a fair share of muscles."

She popped her head out around the side of the canvas with a smile, but I had to keep mine to myself or else. Her face was streaked with a few swipes of paint, the most prominent being the intensely bright green dotted on the tip of her nose.

"I appreciate your cooperation. You will be generously compensated for it." Her head had no sooner disappeared behind the canvas before it popped back out. "And by generously compensated, I mean in sexual favors. Naturally." With a wink, she disappeared again.

As I always did whenever the conversation steered toward that topic, I changed the subject. Quickly. Not because I was one of those guys who got creeped out by the idea of making love to his pregnant wife, but because her heart was already straining enough without the added stress of intimacy. "Do you still want to plan on leaving the city after your appointment tomorrow? Have you had enough time to pack?"

"I am not planning, I am *dying* to leave tomorrow,

and yeah, I've already packed. I'm ready to hit the road. Bags are waiting at the door, and I've got a supply of peanut butter for the road trip. I picked up kale chips and raw walnuts for you."

Last year, I would have laughed if she'd suggested what she just packed for our road trip fuel or even thought about implying a cowboy from Montana knew what kale was . . . but last year felt like a former lifetime. "Yum. You know I can't resist a crunchy-bordering-on-chewy piece of glorified lettuce, and who can say no to unsalted nuts? On second thought, double yum."

That earned a small laugh from her as she worked on the painting. "Come on, it's like I told you. A plate of red meat and bowl of mashed potatoes swimming in cream and butter is no longer considered the height of health food. Sorry. Besides, all we need to do is look to nature to discover how to take care of our bodies. Carrots are good for our eyes—cut one section off, and you can see it actually looks like an eye. Tomatoes are good for our hearts—cut one down the center, and you can see chambers and ventricles and pretty much a human heart drawn in nature. Crack into a walnut shell, and what does it look like? A brain, just like what it's good for. More natural foods, less cholesterol and heart disease dripping from a plate please."

I'd heard that lecture countless times in three months, and it still managed to amuse me every time. "If I'm to buy into your theory that we only need to look at what we eat to know what part of our body it's good for, what part of mine is a kale chip benefiting?" I felt my brows draw together as I considered what part of the human anatomy was flat, frilly, and putrid green.

Rowen grumbled from behind the canvas. "Those

gifts from nature that don't resemble anything inside our bodies mean they're good for our *entire* body."

"My butter-laden mashed potatoes don't resemble anything in the human anatomy. So I'm going to infer, based on your conclusion, that eating a serving or five at each sitting is beneficial for my whole body."

Another grumble, that one louder. These were the moments that got me through our impasse in life. The light ones tempered with laughter and each of us trying to outdo and one up the other. We'd talked so much heavy lately, pertaining to a topic that was heavy in the way that leaned toward the doom-and-gloom end of the spectrum, I clung onto any chance for light and fun and laughter for as long as possible. It wasn't just good for me; I knew it was good for her too.

"No, mashed potatoes *do* look like something inside your body," she said in a tone that gave away nothing. "Your heart after it explodes from clogging and contaminating it with saturated fats and empty carbs."

I laughed, loud enough for her to hear, but she must have thought I'd earned one since I didn't get a reprimand for breaking composure. Her laugh joined with mine, along with the sounds of her brush strokes and dabs.

You see, my health was Rowen's thing. Her habit or fixation or whatever-have-you that had cropped up in the wake of all of this uncertainty was her interest-slash-bordering-on-obsession with keeping me healthy. The food thing was where it had started and was most obvious. Breakfasts of eggs, bacon, and buttered toast had been replaced with steel-cut oats mixed with cinnamon and raisins, served alongside an unpalatable heap of runny egg whites (no salt, of course). On the days I worked, she'd taken to packing me lunches instead of letting me pack my own or, heaven forbid, stop by one of those express-line-to-the-morgue places the rest of the world called drive-thrus. Dinner had turned into a ritual of packing as many vitamins, micro-nutrients, and healthy proteins as she could get into me . . . which translated to me forcing each bite down as I held a careful smile in place and praised her efforts high and low. It was a good thing it was my mouth doing the praising and not my stomach though. It didn't know what to do with things like mustard greens and seared ahi and goji berries. It had been fed ranch food for two decades and wasn't accepting the diet change with good grace.

The Keep Jesse Healthy agenda didn't start and end with the food thing though. No, that was just where it dug its heels in. Rowen had started collecting vials of essential oils and mixing them into what I think she called a diffuser at night to help me fall asleep and stay asleep, and she'd taken to rubbing a potent concoction of oregano oil into the bottoms of my feet every day to supposedly up my immune system.

She'd also found a doctor for me, scheduled an appointment, and pretty much ordered a full panel work-up of my blood tests so nothing could slip through the cracks, not even my slightly elevated levels of cholesterol. You should have seen the meals that week following the blood results. I was pretty sure my stomach lining was still trying to repair itself.

I didn't have to ask her why that was the thing she'd latched onto—making sure I stayed healthy. I knew. She wanted to make sure our baby would have at least one healthy parent to see them through a good part of their life.

One parent who'd see them through their formative years and hopefully way beyond. I tried not to think about that or give any indication that I'd connected those dots. Rowen had a right to her idiosyncrasies; God knew I had my share of mine.

"Can you believe Garth?" she said suddenly, breaking a few minutes of silence. "It's a miracle. A miracle among other miracles."

I had to consciously clear my head in order to respond. "Yeah, I know. I can't believe he made a full recovery."

"Oh, not that. Though I guess that's a miracle of sorts too." Her brush stopped before her bare feet took a few steps back to inspect the painting. "The miracle I'm talking about is the one having to do with him finally proposing to Josie and quite possibly the even bigger one of her agreeing to marry him."

The longer she stared at the painting, the more her left foot rose up onto its toes, twisting on its ball. That was something she did, unconsciously I was certain, whenever she inspected something she was working on. I didn't mention anything about it because I thought it was pretty damn adorable, and I kind of liked knowing something about her that even she wasn't aware of. Her toenail color changed on a regular basis, no color too bright or unconscionable for her. I'd started to pick up that her nail polish color went with her mood for the day or week.

Since she'd arrived at Willow Springs and spent the first half of the summer with black nails and toes, I probably should have picked up on that theme earlier, but I had an excuse for being a little slow on the uptake—I was a guy.

Today though, she'd painted her toes a screaming bright orange so vivid I wasn't sure the most tropical of sunsets could ever match its hue. Last week it had been a sparkly teal, almost identical to the flashy bass boat a certain Mason brother owned and had tried to invite me out on the last time I was in town. I might have liked to fish and I might have liked to fish for bass, but my family would have to be starving with no other option for food before I'd climb into a boat with Colt Mason and spend a day fishing with him. It took one full, clearing breath to rid my mind of Colt Mason before I could rejoin the conversation. From peanut butter to miracles to toenails to Colt Mason. I was all over the board tonight.

"Garth's wanted to marry Josie since the day he saw her." I stopped to clear my throat when I could still hear the stirrings of resentment in my voice. The mere thought of Colt Mason made my blood boil in about two seconds flat, and it wasn't in a hurry to cool down either. "That's not that hard for me to believe."

Rowen's foot continued to rise up onto her toes and twist to some imaginary beat. "Yeah, but how long's he wanted to and not done anything about it? Garth's too much like me—we don't like to believe we're worthy of the things we want most. He's even worse than I am actually. That's why it's a miracle he proposed to her."

I noticed her elbows stab up into the air for a few moments before they fell back at her sides, leaving behind a paintbrush, bristles still dribbling paint, pointing toward the sky. When rubber bands were in short supply, paintbrushes were a quick and convenient way to get her hair out of her face.

"I'm a bit concerned that you just compared yourself

to Garth," I said.

"What can I say? We're kindred spirits."

My brows hit my hairline. "What am I then? If Garth's your kindred spirit?"

Her foot stopped twisting, and the heel lowered back to the floor. Then her heels clacked together, not three times but two. That meant she liked what she'd just inspected with a scrupulous eye. I'd picked up on lots of things I'd never noticed about Rowen—kind of a side effect of being afraid to blink when she was close by.

Done with her heel clicking ritual, she came around the side of the canvas. On her face was a smile . . . and paint. Lots of paint. I couldn't tell if she'd mistaken her forehead for the canvas instead of the four-by-four foot thing I'd spent countless hours staring at the back of. I had to rub at my mouth to keep her from picking up on my grin, but really, it was impossible to look at her speckled and splattered face looking like a rainbow had just dried itself all over her without smiling.

If she noticed, she didn't say anything. Instead she held her smile in place and moved toward me, intention filling her eyes. "My soul mate."

I stopped trying to hide my smile and waved her closer.

"You feel better now?" she asked. "Or are you still put out I suggested Garth and I are kindred spirits?"

I'd been too busy staring at her face to notice that it wasn't the only part of her marked and dotted with color. She was wearing one of my big white shirts, which she'd taken to wearing to bed after her stomach started to stretch through her own sleep tanks and tees. When she'd first slid into one of my shirts a month ago, she'd looked as though she could have gone parachuting in it. The bottom had just barely cleared her knees. Slowly though, day after day, I'd watched that shirt creep higher and higher up her legs as her stomach grew. By the end, the fabric would be stretched and pulled across that part of her where it still hung, but I could just make out the faintest of swells if I looked really close.

I loved her in my old shirts. I loved that she wore them to sleep in. I loved that within the confines of that cotton was the woman I loved and the baby we'd created as a result of that love.

So that was what I attempted to focus on when she folded herself into the chair with me, wiggling and twisting until she found just the right position on my lap. I didn't think about her sick heart, which was also inhabiting that space. That same heart that threatened to take my family away from me in one tragic moment.

"I feel better now," I answered at last, winding my arms around her as I tucked my chin over the top of her head. My response had less to do with what she'd said and more to do with having her in my arms. She knew that too.

We sat like that for a moment, her running her fingers up and down the back of my forearm for so long that I felt a wave of sleepiness hit me. The moment she stirred in my lap, that passed.

"I still can't believe he tried that thing with Colt though." She shook her head against my chest. "I don't know if I've ever seen Josie so pissed. And I've seen her pissed. A lot. In fact, I think that might be her favorite emotion. It's her most convincing one at least."

That blood-boiling sensation flooded back in full force. It didn't even need two seconds to achieve maximum lift-off. “He can try to set Colt up with the rest of the town for all I care.” I glared through the window across from us. “Just so long as it doesn’t involve my family.”

“I take it from that tone and steely expression that you haven’t gotten over Colt Mason being Lily’s boyfriend?”

“He’s not her boyfriend,” I said, feeling my jaw lock into place at the thought of Lily being Colt’s . . . *girlfriend.* “They’re dating. They’ve been *on* dates. That’s it.” My fists were curling. “That’s enough.” All I could see was Colt and Lily together, talking, touching . . . “*More* than enough.”

“It didn’t seem like you had the see-red bug at the thought of Colt that Garth had a while ago.” She lifted her head off of my chest to look at me, but I just kept glaring out that window.

“That was before he decided to ask my little sister, who happens to be way younger than him, out on a date.” My eyes narrowed a fraction more. “That’s bad form. Where I come from, that’s not the way we do it. Since Colt’s got about as much country in him as he’s got honor, I guess I shouldn’t have expected him to follow the same code.”

“Is Garth channeling you right now?” She shifted a bit, framing my face with her fingers and squeezing one of her eyes shut as she focused on me. “Because I swear to God what you just said, in that same exact self-righteous-meets-self-loathing tone he’s perfected, with that so-close-it’s-seriously-freaking-me-out expression . . . Garth, are you in there?” She stopped framing my face long enough to knock on my forehead. “Don’t make me perform an exorcism because, so help me god, I will if you do not leave my sweet, accepting, thoughtful husband alone. Be gone, evil spirit," she said with a palm shoved into my forehead.

Winding my fingers around her wrists, I lowered them back into her lap. Although her lap had changed. The soft flatness of it had been exchanged for a rounded firmness that still made me almost jump when I felt it without thinking. Instead of letting my hands slip away, Rowen grabbed my wrists and settled my hands on her stomach. After spreading my fingers on both hands, she smiled down at the picture. I studied the same image and smiled too—my smile was just more touched with sadness than hers.

My view had changed too. When she'd first started framing her stomach with my hands, all of my fingers had overlapped. By a lot at first, then less and less. I liked being able to look down and see that—my hands on her, my fingers touching, almost as if I could keep all of us together. Last week, my fingers had stopped touching, and yet another, albeit misplaced, sentiment of control slipped out of my grasp and another thimble of hope drained out of my bucket.

It had the opposite effect on Rowen though. My fingers being unable to touch seemed to be some kind of landmark to her. Something to celebrate.

Looking down, I saw a noticeable difference in how far apart they were this week over last. That would be the trend from here on out though. Each week, each day, this would slip further and further out of my grasp. I couldn't keep us all together and safe. I couldn't catch her or the baby if they fell. I couldn't protect them if I couldn't reach them. Even as I stared at her stomach, my hands framed around it, I realized what an odd thought that was to have, but acknowledging that didn't lessen the reality of what I was feeling. Unfortunately.

"Okay, okay, so enough with the Garth-channeling jokes." She fitted her hands on either side of mine, so they made one small circle around her stomach. "What's this code you're talking about though? Is it one you can share with, you know, a girl? One who was raised in the, gasp, city of all places?"

From the corner of my eye, I saw her smirking at me, but I couldn't seem to tear my gaze away from her stomach and our hands circled around it. "It's not a code, per se, but it's something Colt would have a basic understanding of if he'd been born and raised the way I had."

She nudged her pinkie into my thumb. "Am I to infer from that vague explanation that you're saying Colt should have known better than to ask out a friend's sister?"

"Exactly."

She nodded slowly, swinging her legs over the arm of the chair; those glaring orange toes flashed at me. "But don't you all kind of grow up knowing each other, being from a small dot on the map and putting so much importance on helping each other out? Wouldn't you, if you wanted to date someone in the same zip code as you, kind of have to ask out some friend's sister eventually?"

I wanted to answer with a quick and adamant no, but I couldn't. Because she was right. Back where I came from, plenty of friends dated plenty of friends' sisters, so I didn't know why I was so worked up over Colt and Lily. The age difference had something to do with it, but it wasn't as though he were fifty and asking her out. I don't think it was his family's money or where they had ties to. So what did I have so against Colt Mason dating my sister?

I'd been trying to figure that out for a while and had come up empty, so I answered Rowen's questions with a long sigh.

"What are you going to do if you see them together at Garth and Josie's engagement party this weekend?" she asked. "Can you be civil? Not manage to embarrass your sister like you did when we ran into them at the movie theater last time we were in town?"

"They were all over each other," I argued.

Rowen squeezed her fingers tied through mine. "They were holding hands."

I huffed and shifted my gaze between our combined hands and her stomach. "Yeah, and look where holding hands got us."

Her eyebrow lifted. "Happy? Married? In love?" She let that soak in. "Wouldn't you want the same for your sister?"

"Of course that's what I want for Lily. I want that for all of my sisters."

Rowen was waiting with a *well, then* look on her face.

"I'd just rather they not find it with any of the Mason brothers."

She laughed. "Well in our perfect world, I'll make sure that happens, but in this world, maybe you can figure out a way to accept it." As soon as my mouth flew open, she added, "Or at least *deal* with it. For your sister. You know how much Lily looks up to you and wants your approval."

I grumbled to myself, a habit I'd taken up ever since I found out about Lily and Colt. "Yeah, well, she obviously wasn't looking for my approval on this."

"No, but I bet she wouldn't mind having it."

I gave my thoughts to that with another huff.

"So moving on from that topic that stresses you out like nothing else . . ." Rowen wiggled farther down in my lap, her eyes drooping with sleep's call. "You all set for tomorrow's appointment? After the last one, I almost asked the doctor if he could prescribe an anti-anxiety pill I could force-feed you an hour before the ultrasounds."

My mouth went dry thinking about her appointment. Since Rowen was in the high-risk category, we'd been having ultrasounds at all of our monthly appointments, and she was right—every one had been like a slow form of torture. Waiting for the tech to find the baby, then find the heartbeat . . . that was the worst. Waiting to hear that flutter of a heartbeat echoing through the room. I knew it was Rowen who had the heart condition, but I'd somehow projected that onto the baby, and half the time, I was worried that our child's heart would give out too. It probably had something to do with knowing that if Rowen's gave out with the baby in her stomach, so would our child's. Morbid thoughts hadn't been in short supply the past few months. They were either haunting me or I was haunting them. I couldn't tell.

"Yeah, that isn't exactly a less stressful topic to discuss actually." I couldn't keep from smiling as I watched her eyes fade a bit more as she slumped in my arms. Pregnancy had turned Rowen into a champion at falling asleep quickly. "But yeah, I'm as ready as I ever am before our appointments."

"I know they're hard on you." She was interrupted by a yawn. "You don't have to go to every one, you know? In case you haven't noticed, you're usually the only guy camped out beside a pregnant woman in the waiting room, so you don't have to feel guilty for missing a couple of appointments. It might be good for you to take a break."

I drew my thumb down her cheek, cutting a line through the still-wet streaks of paint. "You don't get to take a break. I don't either then."

"Yeah, but I'm not the one who's about to have a heart attack every time we go." It was barely recognizable, but something registered on her expression. She caught what she'd said but wouldn't, for the life of her, admit it.

I hadn't missed it either. Turning my thumb over, I saw the paint had transferred to my skin. A swirl of colors had seeped into the whorls of my fingerprint. I stared at it, wondering how something so beautiful could just be scrubbed away. Gone forever. As if it had never been there to start with. "I want to go. I like to go. I'm just terrified at the same time."

Rowen was in the middle of a yawn, but she cut it in half. Her hand molded into the bend of my neck. I hadn't realized how cool I'd been until I felt her warmth bleeding into my skin. "It'll be okay. We've made it this far. I've stayed healthy. The baby is healthy. We're in the homestretch." She smiled, waiting for me to mirror it. It didn't come easily or naturally, but I managed it. I could manage anything for her. "Nothing left to worry about but how to stockpile diapers and keep ourselves sane during the first crazy year."

We *were* nearing the homestretch: the last few months leading up to the delivery and the most physically taxing part of the entire pregnancy. The most stressful, straining endeavor a woman could go through. How would her heart handle it? *Could* it handle it?

For Rowen, every day that passed eased her worries. It was the opposite for me.

CHAPTER two

Rowen

I MIGHT HAVE been the pregnant one, but it was as if Jesse was the one sitting on a ticking time bomb. From the time we rolled into my OB-GYN's office and plopped into a couple of chairs, his left leg hadn't stopped bouncing. Although bouncing wasn't exactly the right word for it because it was moving so quickly, it was almost a blur from the corner of my eyes. If the nurse didn't pop her head through that door soon and call my name, he would rub a patch of the low-pile carpet bald with the heel of his boot. Along with the lacquer coating the wood chair-arm he kept running his hand over, twisting and squeezing it like he was trying to rein it into submission.

His other hand was holding mine, and it was as steady and solid as I was used to when it came to Jesse. He had my hand gathered in his without a trace of that anxiety he had so bottled up inside it was about to explode all over the place. Like his hand holding mine, his leg skimming my leg was still and sure. The half of Jesse closest to me gave no indication that the man inside was falling apart, but the other half, the one farthest from me, looked as if it had staged war on him.

It was a phenomenon I'd gotten used to over the past few months. Ever since I'd flashed those pink lines in his face and he'd looked as though I'd pointed at my obituary in the newspaper instead. That pregnancy stick had been like a death sentence in Jesse's eyes, and each day that followed only brought me closer to my date with the hereafter. He'd never said that in so many words, but he didn't have to. His whole body said it. Or at least the half of his body that was just out of my reach.

"Hey, Jesse?" I gave his hand a little squeeze while I snagged the sandwich bag nestled inside my purse. "Maybe you should have some of this before we get called back there."

Jesse's eyes flitted to the door where the nurses called us back as if behind that door was a portal of no return. I had to wave the sandwich in front of his face before his stare could be broken.

"You made me a sandwich?" he said in a voice I'd gotten used to. It still sounded the same, but Jesse's clear, smooth tone had been roughed up by stress and sleepless nights. His words came out sounding like they'd been rolled in gravel now. "You're the one who's pregnant, and you made *me* a sandwich?" When a sigh slipped out, it gave an indication of just how exhausted he was. That sigh made it sound like he hadn't slept in months . . . which might not have been a stretch. "I should be the one making you sandwiches. Not the other way around. Why didn't I think of that?"

Since the sandwich was still hanging in front of his face, I pulled out one of the halves and had to curl his hand around it. "Hmmm, I don't know. Maybe because you were busy thinking about getting the truck loaded with all of our luggage, and worrying about every facial expression I made after eating too many pancakes and mistaking indigestion with sudden onslaught death?" When his head whipped in my direction, all I did was arch an eyebrow. His expression led me to the conclusion he wasn't thrilled with my word choice. "Or maybe because you've been busy hovering over me, trying to predict my every need and want, along with trying to keep up with work while keeping our condo so clean and tidy dust and debris don't dare think to cover one of the surfaces in Unit 212."

I was looking into his eyes, but it was everything around them I was really noticing. Shadows had been under his eyes for weeks now, for so long it was as if those dark hollows had become permanent fixtures. Even his skin color had faded a shade or two. The hint of bronze that even a couple of long Seattle gray-skied winters couldn't touch had been erased by a few months of his wife's pregnancy. He still shaved every morning, but the small nicks and cuts he left behind told the story of a man going through the motions while his mind was weighed down with worry. The corners of his eyes were perhaps what I noticed most. Even when I woke up in the middle of the night to pee for the one hundredth time and he looked as close to asleep as Jesse got these days, the corners of those eyes were still creased. Three little lines stemmed from the corners of his eyes and stretched out to touch his temples.

It was clear he was worried about me.

I was just as worried about him.

"You eat it." Jesse nodded at the sandwich still hanging in front of his face. "You need it more than I do. I'm not hungry anyway."

I kept half-waving the sandwich in front of his face. "You haven't been hungry since you know when, so if you'd been following your eat-when-I'm-hungry compass, you'd be a runway model in cowboy boots right now."

He eyed the sandwich but wasn't taking the nutrition bait. I wasn't exaggerating that I'd all but force-fed him for three months. If I didn't set something in front of him or remind him or, on some days, *order* him to eat, it would have slipped his mind entirely. That was how distracted he'd been.

"Come on, I'll eat the other half if you eat this half," I said.

Sometimes a compromise was the only way I got through to him. They said compromise was the key to any successful relationship . . . I just never imagined that meant divvying up an organic peanut butter and all-fruit spread sandwich in a gynecologist's waiting room so my husband wouldn't pass out from lack of sustenance.

Jesse took the sandwich half and nodded. "Deal." He waited to dive in until I'd freed my half from the baggie and had sunk my teeth into it.

I wasn't hungry. My stomach was still swimming with pancake, but if that was the only way to get him to eat, I could suck it up. He'd barely managed to get down one pancake that morning, and I hadn't pushed him on it because I knew how nervous these appointments made him. The only reason I was pushing the PB&J issue was because I was worried he'd go into hypoglycemic shock or something if he didn't get something in his system. All of that stress and the way it manifested in bouncy legs and twitchy hands had a way of eating into a person's energy reserves.

We nibbled at the corners of our sandwiches in silence. That was something else that had taken some getting used to—the silence. Not just any kind of silence, but the kind I was acutely aware of. Jesse and I had been comfortable in the quiet places from the start of our relationship and had never felt the urge to fill a peaceful moment with mindless chatter, but this silence was different. Not exactly awkward, but noticeable. I preferred our shared silences to pass so naturally I didn't even realize they were happening. Our quiet moments together didn't pass effortlessly anymore.

I was halfway done with my sandwich half when a couple staggered into the office, both yawning. The guy carried a car seat with a sleeping infant who couldn't have been older than a week or two. "Zombies" was the term that came to my mind as they shuffled up to the check-in desk before dragging themselves toward a free row of chairs and collapsing into them. The baby was asleep because he or she was tired from keeping the parents up all night. I didn't think the mom had finished her yawn before she fell asleep with her head draped across her husband's shoulder.

I nudged Jesse's leg with mine and indicated the new family. "That's what we have to look forward to in a few short months. You up for it?" I had to wrestle with my smile when the man broke into a snore chorus that sounded like he was wrestling with an unruly chainsaw.

I guessed Jesse hadn't noticed them when they'd first staggered in, because when his gaze lifted to them, he studied the family as if he was seeing them for the first time. For a moment, the corners of his eyes ironed out. That almost peaceful expression didn't last long though.

Not even long enough for me to hope that once this was all over, that look would return.

"I would *love* to look forward to that actually," he said softly, studying them as though he wasn't just seeing the big picture but the fine details too. The things most people missed when they looked at others.

I didn't miss his use of the word would, as if being exhausted and sporting two different-colored socks like the dad camped out in a waiting room wasn't a guarantee for us . . . but I also knew better than to call him on it. I'd spent two months calling him out on those kinds of comments before realizing that he might retract his statement and try to get me to believe that wasn't how he meant it, but all it took was one look in his eyes to find the truth. Jesse was entitled to his worries, as I was entitled to mine. I just did a better job of hiding mine than he did his, and that was why he hadn't noticed. I was glad he hadn't noticed because here was the thing—I worried about him, but he was already so worried about me that if he knew I was nearing freak-out zones like he was, it would only make his anxiety chart new levels of unhealthy. So I kept my worries to myself.

Jesse had been the strong one for me in so many things. I could return the favor this time.

"So?" I checked the time on the clock behind the reception desk for the who-knew-what-number-of-times since we'd arrived almost an hour ago. "Since it would appear Dr. Stuart is delivering yet another baby at this month's scheduled appointment time, have your views on the whole name thing changed? We've got time to kill and nothing to fill it with unless you want to read about how to make the perfect four-layer cake." I eyed the magazine sitting on one of the chairs beside us.

Jesse shook his head. "No." It kept shaking. "I'm not ready to go over names, Rowen. I'm sorry. Just . . . not yet." His bouncing leg froze when I suggested the name thing, but it had just restarted and was moving double-time.

"You've been saying that since I dropped that dictionary-sized baby name book in front of you right after finding out I was pregnant. When do you think you'll be ready?"

He set his half-eaten sandwich on his leg. "I don't know. I just know I'm not ready right this minute."

"We're running out of minutes before this little thing in my stomach will be out of said stomach, and it would be nice if we had a few names to choose from before we leave the hospital with Baby Sterling-Walker on the birth certificate." I stuffed what was left of the sandwich back in the baggie. We'd choked down enough. "Although the upside to that name is that one day we might get to experience some strapping young rebel marching up to us and saying, "Nobody puts Baby in a corner," before whisking her away to a stage and iconic eighties movie glory."

Jesse wasn't smiling. Not even a hint of one. Either he'd totally missed my Jennifer-Garner-meets-Patrick-Swayze reference or he didn't find it funny. At least I did.

"Come on, Jesse. What is it? What's the thing about the names that's so hard for you?"

His gaze flickered to my stomach, making the lines at the corners of his eyes etch deeper. "It's just too much like . . . I don't know, inviting tragedy or something." He swallowed, not blinking as he studied my stomach. "Talking about names before it's here or before we know what's going to happen . . ." He let the silence fill in the dot, dot, dot because neither of us needed to hear the words. They played on repeat through our minds every day. "If we decide on a name and start referring to it by name, then . . ." He paused to swallow. "Then . . ." It didn't look like any number of swallows could get him past the ball sitting in his throat.

"Then what you're so terrified of happening does, and you don't just lose a Rowen but you lose a Michael or a Michelle too?" I twisted in my seat to face him, holding tightly to his hand.

He couldn't look at me, he couldn't make words come to the surface, but he nodded.

"That's why you don't want to know the gender of the baby, isn't it? Because the less you know about it, the less hard it will be if . . . you know?"

He was still staring at the ground, but I didn't miss the flash that tore through his eyes, almost as if he was ready to tear whatever dared threaten his family's lives limb from limb. "Nothing would make that any less hard. Nothing." Letting go of my hand, he clasped his hands in front of him and leaned forward in his chair.

Since he had his hat on, I couldn't see his face from that angle, but I didn't have to. His back was so tense, I could see the ridge running down the center of it through his shirt. I leaned down beside him, but my stomach got in the way. "Then what is it?"

"It's nothing."

"If it was nothing, we wouldn't be having this conversation."

His knuckles were white, his eyes narrowed at the floor. For a second it looked like he was going to answer, but that changed instantly.

"Come on. You can't keep all of this bottled up or you're going to explode. You need to vent a little sometimes. You need to talk to me, Jesse. I can't help you if you won't be open with me."

"I'm supposed to be helping you, not the other way around," he replied in that rough voice he'd taken on recently.

"Oh, yeah? Where did you read that? The Unhealthy Relationship Bible?" I nudged him with my elbow. "Come on, I can take it. Whatever you have to say, I promise. I know I might seem fragile and emotional, but those are the out-of-whack hormones talking." I dropped my hand on his leg, above his knee. "Come on. Give it to me."

"I can't."

I watched the sleeping-slash-snoring family sitting across from us. I wondered if they'd had to go through the same kinds of obstacles to wind up where they were—together. A step above comatose, but still a family. I couldn't look at them for long without feeling that hole in my stomach start to open. The one I'd told Jesse nothing about because if he knew I was worried about me and the baby making it through this thing, unlike I let on, he wouldn't make it through the next three months without suffering a nervous breakdown.

"Come on, if you don't tell me, I'll assume the worst," I continued, having to sit back up. Leaning forward with a hard beach ball in the way couldn't be endured for very long. "And you know me, I can assume *the* very worst. I have an imagination that knows no bounds. Curse of the artistic types." My eyebrows pulled together. "Well, one of them at least."

My attempts at pleading and rationalizing the truth out of him didn't seem to be working. I was just preparing to go to phase two and plaster on a face he couldn't say no to—at least not for very long—when he shifted, and a few words tumbled from his mouth. "It's this dream." His voice was quiet. "I seem to have it every time I fall asleep. That's why I've been having a tough time sleeping."

"You've been having an impossible time sleeping," I said gently.

"Not that it really matters much, because even if I'm not dreaming it, I can't forget about that dream for very long."

"So it's a nightmare?" I checked the clock again, and this time, instead of wishing the nurse would call my name already, I found myself hoping she wouldn't. Not when he was finally opening up.

His head shook. "Nightmares aren't like this. You wake up from a nightmare and know it was a nightmare, but this . . . this seems real. I can smell things, feel things, taste things. This isn't like any other dream where only one or two senses are involved—in this, I can feel everything." He was still leaning forward, so I couldn't see his face, but I knew enough about that tone to picture his expression.

"What's it about?" I asked, trying to sound as matter-of-fact as I was capable of. Jesse was no stranger to bad dreams, and I didn't want to be responsible for bringing more into his life.

He took two long breaths before he could answer. "It's just me wandering around at night in some large empty field I don't recognize." One of his shoulders quivered. "I'm walking around trying to find you, but I can't. So I start running around, screaming your name, and that's when I trip over something." His back rose and fell. "That's when I see the headstones. Your name is on one, but the name on the one beside yours is blurry. I can't make it out."

Jesse managed to keep his voice level, his breathing even. I was able to do the same, but only because I was working really hard to stay calm. Nothing about what he was saying bred calm.

"Whenever I reach out to rub at the name, to try to see the letters, that's when I'm jerked awake. Not wanting to see that name is what snaps me out of that place, and that's why I don't want to decide on names." Finally, he looked at me over his shoulder. His eyes were bloodshot from lack of sleep, and there wasn't a square inch of his face that didn't show the wear and tear of the months of self-torture, but still, he managed to work a smile into place for me. A real smile that reminded me of the first time we met and how curious it had seemed to me at the time that someone could smile so effortlessly and mean it.

"You're afraid that if you see that name on the headstone, you won't be able to wake yourself up?" I dropped my hand to his neck and combed my fingers into the light hair at the base of his neck.

His head shook once. "I'm afraid that if we name our baby before it's born, death will have an easier time finding it."

I nearly choked on the ball that had decided to take residence in the middle of my throat. It came out of nowhere, derived from emotions that extended past understanding. I felt the same sorrow I supposed he did every time he relived his dream. I felt my own worry dial up a few notches when I thought of everything we had ahead of us. But I also felt relief. It was a strange emotion in the lineup, but it was the only welcome one.

Jesse tipped his head at me, leaning back in his seat. "Why do you look like all of your worries are gone?"

I guessed the relief was what manifested on my face. "Because this whole time, I thought you didn't want to know the gender of the baby or discuss names because you wanted to keep your distance from it." I had to clear my throat before I could say anything else. "I thought it might have been because you were upset . . . resentful . . . of what might happen to me."

Jesse's face softened before I could finish my sentence. Then his arm went around my shoulders, and he gently guided my head to his shoulder. "I'm sorry you felt that way. Although I suppose it's not too hard to understand why you felt that way. I have been removed and keeping my distance from the baby, but not because of my lack of feelings for it. It's because of my abundance of them."

His voice was so strong and soothing in my ear, I found myself closing my eyes and basking in it like the first warm rays of sunshine after a long, hard Montana winter.

"I've been afraid that whatever it is out there that seems intent to even the scales when someone experiences more happiness than the average person should will rush in and rectify that. I'm worried that I've lived so many happy moments that I've hit some lifetime limit and they're all going to disappear." He sighed then kissed my temple. "I'm worrying because that's all it feels like I can control with this. I've gotten really good at it too."

Given the conversation, I knew I shouldn't feel continued relief. I accepted that in most instances, a pregnant wife would be freaked out if her husband had just told her about a recurring hellish nightmare he'd been having and his premonitions about life evening the scales. But I didn't. I felt as if I'd been climbing a mountain with a giant pack strapped to my back, and it had been pulled off and I'd finally scaled the summit.

"I wish you would have told me this earlier. That's a heavy burden to bear all on your own." When I breathed in, I smelled his favorite soap on him, and the world felt a little more right again.

"You're telling me I've got a heavy burden to bear? I'm not the one with a living thing growing inside me."

He was trying to get me to laugh. It worked. "So I've got the physical burden to bear, but you've got the mental one. It would make it a lot easier if we helped each other out with of our burdens. Don't you think?" When he didn't answer right away, I added, "Come on, no fair. You've helped me with my burden so much." I highlighted my stomach with my hands. "I know you've thought about carrying me down the hall or up the stairs or through the store, but you know better than to try it because there'd be no end to my wrath. But you make more meals these days than I do, give me nightly back rubs, and you got that cocoa butter stuff for my stomach to prevent the stretch marks I was worried about, so now all I'll have to worry about is a giant incision scar running down my lower abdomen." I was hoping to pull a laugh from him, but no dice. "You've helped me the whole time. Let me help you now too."

The baby curled up in its car seat across from us

woke up and started to make the tiniest little cries mixed with coos. No joke, the passed out parents snapped awake as if a tub of ice water had been poured over their heads. Both of them reached for the baby like it was an involuntary reflex, but in the process, they managed to bonk their heads together. It barely slowed them down though. The sleepy-eyed dad chuckled and gave his head a rub, letting the yawning mom who'd issued an *oww!* wind the baby out of the car seat.

It was like a not-so-carefully orchestrated dance. They moved together in an undesignated way, but somehow, it all worked. They were a family. They had only been one for maybe a week but were already working together in such harmony that it struck me how adaptable we humans could be, and how we were wired to form bonds and connections.

I was still staring at the exhausted, happy family when the nurse called my name. From the look on her face, it wasn't the first time she'd called it either.

Jesse was already up, extending his hand for me to take. When I did, he pulled me up smoothly, draped an arm around my shoulders, and guided me to where the nurse's frown had turned upside down. I took one more glance over my shoulder at the family, emotion burning my throat. I wanted that bad.

"How are you feeling, Rowen?" The nurse held her smile as Jesse and I passed through the door.

"Like I'm a giant petri dish." I generally spewed those kinds of comments to get a smile or chuckle from Jesse—he'd needed every one I could pull out of him lately—but he was in another world and tiny beads of sweat were starting to dot his temples.

The nurse definitely caught my comment though. She tilted her head back at me, her shoes continuing to squeak down the hall. "A petri dish?"

I shrugged and eyed my stomach. "I feel like my sole purpose right now is to let this little thing grow."

Her smile was definitely forced as she turned into one of the rooms. I supposed she was probably used to expectant mothers answering her with phrases like *Not bad* or *Pretty Good* or maybe even *Really pregnant*, but she hadn't asked someone else—she'd asked me. I felt like a petri dish.

"We're going to have Ben do your ultrasound, then Doctor Stuart will see you." The nurse lifted her head at the tech in the corner, who flashed us a wave before scanning my chart. "You already gave a urine sample, correct?"

My bladder felt like it had the stamina of a ninety-five-year-old woman instead of a girl in her twenties. I could barely make it through the trailers at a movie before having to waddle for the bathrooms.

I nodded. "The highlight of my day. Peeing into a cup and passing it between a double door."

Forced smile number two. Man, either I was off my game or Mrs. Stiff Lip wouldn't even find Taylor Swift rapping while tap-dancing in a straitjacket funny.

"Ben will make sure you get to a patient room when your ultrasound's complete." The nurse hustled through the door, closing it, and went on to spread her merriment through the rest of the office.

"Hey, Ben," I said, already peeling my oversized band shirt over my head. I'd been through the ultrasound-slash-examine routine enough to have it memorized.

"How's it going?"

When the room stayed quiet, after tossing my shirt onto the empty chair in the corner, I glanced around. First at Jesse. Then at Ben. Both had varying shades of discomfort coloring their faces.

"Oh, right. Sorry." I snagged the thin cotton dress from the exam table and unfolded it. "Exhibitionism is a tough habit to break."

Ben was a special shade of pink as he hopped off his stool and powered toward the door, his eyes cast down. "I'll give you a few minutes to change and then I'll be back."

When the door closed, I finished peeling off what was left, ignoring Jesse waiting for me to look at him. The last time Dr. Stuart had been out sick and a different doctor, a male one, had to do my exam, I thought I would have to duct tape Jesse into the corner when the doctor did the internal pelvic exam. Jesse had never been a jealous man who was threatened by other guys in my life, but I supposed that ended when someone started touching me down there. Even if that someone was an M.D. and touched so many "down theres" on a daily basis he was totally desensitized about the whole thing.

"Stop looking at me like I just committed murder." When I slid out of my panties, I sling-shotted them in his direction. They hit his stomach. Bull's-eye.

Jesse caught my underwear before they fell to the floor, and he watched me as I tied the gown. "Maybe next time you could refrain from stripping until the just-earned-the-right-to-order-a-beer-in-a-bar male is out of the room?" He folded the rest of my clothes and placed them on the counter.

"Oh, please. He works in an OB-GYN office. He's seen more naked ladies and had his magic wand up more women's hoo-haws than the lead singer of the boy band I refuse to name out loud."

Jesse slid the chair across the room, shaking his head. "You're probably right, but he hasn't seen *my* wife's naked body or . . ." Jesse's gaze shifted to the ultrasound machine, where the torture-looking device also known as an intra-uterine ultrasound device was hanging. The first couple of ultrasounds had been way less pleasant. "That other part, so sorry if I'm a little uncomfortable with you exposing yourself in front of some other guy."

"Exposing myself? I think we've got a rather large difference in the definition of that term."

After sliding the chair up beside the exam table, he headed to the sink. "You took off your shirt."

I could tell from his tone and expression that he wasn't really upset. When Jesse was really upset, I could see the ridge running down his jaw pop to the surface of his skin. "I was wearing a bra, in case you didn't notice."

He filled one of those tiny paper cups with water and emptied it before looking back. Half of his mouth was turned up. "Yeah, but it's my favorite bra. I don't want to share it with some other guy."

If I'd had another pair of panties in my hand, I would have flung them at him too. But the bull's-eye would have been his face. "Are you done acting like a crazy person for the day?"

That was when the tech knocked on the door before opening it a hair. "All set in here?"

Jesse's face went two shades paler.

"Okay, so not *quite* done acting like a crazy person," I

muttered before throwing the door open and waving the tech inside. "Ready, and sorry for the earlier strip tease. Everyone tells me I don't have much of a filter, and I guess that also applies to changing into an exam dress."

The tech still looked a shade red, but he went another one at the term "strip tease." After muttering a quick, "No problem," he hustled around the table toward the machine. He couldn't make eye contact with me.

I moved onto the exam table and got into position, not waiting for an invitation. The sooner we got it started, the sooner we could have it finished. I didn't have to press my fingers to Jesse's pulse to know his heart was close to exploding out of his chest. As he moved up beside me and settled into the chair, I almost reminded him to take a breath when it looked like he was turning blue. But when I grabbed his hand, he sucked in a heavy breath of air.

"Would you grab the lights for me please?" Ben asked Jesse, who didn't let go of my hand as he stretched toward the wall behind us and flicked them off.

Ben pointed a remote at the big television screen hanging across from us, then he gingerly scooted the folds of my dress aside to expose my stomach. He was careful to make sure his skin didn't touch mine, and from the corner of my eye, I saw Jesse watching him as if he was ready to throw down if Ben got a little fresh with me. Men.

Jesse's hand in mine was twisting and squeezing as if my fingers and palm were his personal stress ball. It wasn't quite painful, but close. However, I didn't say anything because I knew, based on the anxiety ripping through him right now, this little bit of hand-wringing was nothing. At every ultrasound we'd had, Jesse had acted as if he was sitting in the stands while my verdict of guilty or innocent was read in court. He had everything and was terrified he could lose it all with one appointment.

"Do you know the sex of the baby?" Ben asked as he squirted a stream of warm goo onto my stomach.

"No," Jesse and I said in unison.

"Do you want to?"

"No," we said again, though Jesse's voice was more adamant than mine.

Ben nodded, giving us both looks that hinted that he thought we might have been the oddest couple he'd come across. "Okay, then let's see how this little guy or girl is growing."

When he dropped the wand onto my stomach, I heard Jesse suck in a breath and hold it. He wouldn't stop holding it until he saw that fluttering little heart and heard it echoing through the room. My heart was the troublesome one, but for all Jesse was concerned, both the baby's and my hearts were like a miracle every day they kept beating. His hand in mine moved past clammy to sweaty, and just as he was leaning forward in his chair, looking close to falling out of it, we heard it—the baby's heart.

The breath he'd been holding came out as a relieved sigh, while my own relief I kept internalized. I worried about the baby too. Probably as much as he did, but only I knew how much.

His fingers stopped twisting mine, and his sweaty palm went back to clammy. While the heartbeat filled the room, so fast it reminded me of a hummingbird's wings, Ben moved the paddle around until we had a good view of the baby on the screen.

I wasn't the sentimental one, or the overly emotional one, but each and every time I'd seen our baby on that screen—even the first time, when it had looked more like a peanut than a baby—my eyes went all blurry and I felt a little hiccup catch in my chest. It was kind of like magic, though with this kind, there was no sleight of hand or science to explain the spectacle before our eyes. This was the truest form of magic.

Jesse stood and moved toward the screen. Every crease and wrinkle on his face was gone. Even in the dark, I could see how light his eyes were when he glanced back at me. "It's the most beautiful thing I've ever seen."

A tear drained down my temple. I swiped it away before Jesse could notice, but another one leaked out of my other eye. I scrubbed that one away too. I'd cried enough sad tears in my life to know what they felt like. These were the happy kind, the good kind of tears.

I couldn't help it, not even when Ben plucked a tissue out of the box resting on the top of the machine and handed it to me. Seeing the man I loved standing in front of me, utterly in awe of the image of the child we'd made together against every odd known to man, while that little heart thudded with such strength and veracity it didn't seem possible it could ever stop, I became an emotional, overwhelmed mess.

When Jesse turned around and noticed though, I'd blame it all on the hormones.

He pulled his phone out of his back pocket, lifted it in front of the screen, adjusted the focus, and snapped a picture.

"I can print you guys off some pictures," Ben said, giving Jesse an odd look as he snapped another. "That's no problem at all."

Jesse nodded. "Sure. Great. Thanks." He took a few

more pictures, all from the same angle and focus, before lowering his phone. "I just want to capture this moment, right now, and remember it." After tucking the phone back into his pocket, he backed up until he was standing beside me again.

When I could finally tear my gaze from the screen, I looked at him. He was staring at me, his eyes warm and his expression so close to euphoric, I wanted to take my own picture to capture this moment.

"It's such a miracle, isn't it?" He lowered his hand to my forehead and brushed my hair back.

If he kept looking at me like that and saying those kinds of things, I would go through the rest of that box of tissues before we got out of there. A change of mood was needed before I melted into a puddle. Glancing at the screen, I smiled at the picture. "I don't know, it kind of looks like an alien to me." I felt Jesse's stare, that's how potent it was. Lifting my eyes, I grinned at him. "It must take after you."

Even teasing him about our child looking like an alien couldn't dampen his mood. "Didn't you hear what I just said?" His fingers tangled through my hair as his eyes shifted from me to the screen. "That baby is one of the most beautiful things I've ever seen." When he looked at me, he was smiling. "It must take after you."

I didn't know how long we stayed like that, touching each other and shifting glances between one another and our baby, but when the wand moved away from my stomach and the screen went blank, the spell was broken.

Broken but not destroyed.

When the lights flipped on, Ben made a quick escape after uttering a brief formality.

Jesse gave me a look. "See what that bra does to a man?"

I laughed so hard my stomach started shaking, and I felt it vibrating in my toes. Going from the nerves of the waiting room to the awe of the ultrasound to him making jokes about my bra's prowess had taken me for a roller coaster ride I wasn't ready to climb off of anytime soon.

"Well I know what it does to you, and you're the only man I'm concerned with anyway." When I started to sit up, he grabbed my hands and helped pull me up. "Although with the way my girls are growing, they'll be spilling out of this bra, as well as all of my other ones, in a non-sexy way very soon."

Jesse's forehead lined, clearly not picking up on my attempts at subtlety.

"So if you want to take this one for one last spin before it gets stuffed into a plastic storage bin labeled 'Before,' you better not wait too long." When I untied the top part of the exam gown, it was no coincidence.

When his gaze dipped to where my fingers were untying the next section, I saw him swallow. When I skimmed my finger down the center of my chest that was, no joke, twice the size I had before getting knocked up, he stepped toward me.

Another thing that had seemed to double in size since getting preggo—my-eggo? My sexual appetite. Which was really unfortunate timing considering Jesse had pretty much declared a freeze in that department because he was freaked out that the combination of being pregnant and orgasming would send my heart into catastrophic overdrive.

Seeing that look in his eyes though . . . matched with

the way I felt . . . I found myself checking the door to see if there was a lock. Damn.

Not that I would let that stop me.

When he took another step closer, I lowered my feet to the cool floor and stood. A moment later, I was sitting again, though I didn't make a conscious decision to do so.

"Rowen?" Jesse rushed toward me, but not in the same way I'd hoped he would. Instead of hunger pulling at his expression, it was worry.

And denied . . .

"I'm fine," I almost snapped, more because I was frustrated with myself and my overactive hormones and his don't-break-the-ticker-with-sex policy. "I just got up too fast." I wanted to reach for my head when another wave of dizziness hit me, but I knew better. If I grabbed my head and closed my eyes after collapsing back down on the exam table, Jesse would stick his head out that door and holler for a doctor to come STAT.

"Lie back down. I'll get someone." His hands dropped to my shoulders and he started to guide me back down, but I resisted.

"I'm. Fine." I focused on his boots, waiting for them to stop going in and out of focus.

I knew what the feeling was. I'd experienced it before. It was a side effect of having a heart that couldn't deal with too much too fast. The further along I got in the pregnancy, the more frequent the dizzy spells became. Jesse had only been present for a couple of others, but I'd experienced dozens more when he wasn't around. Jesse had brought it up at our last heart doctor appointment, and he'd recommended I take it easy and try to limit sudden moves to a minimum, which I had, but it was getting worse. How could I limit getting up and down to a minimum?

I felt worry flex its bony fingers around my gut and squeeze, but I didn't let it show on my face. Jesse's worry monster was showing enough for the both of us.

"I really think you should lie down," he said, his hands moving all around me as if he couldn't figure out what to do but knew he had to do something.

"And I really think you should calm down before you have the heart attack you're so worried I'll have." I took a slow breath then another. Eventually the dizzy haze burned off and I could make out the stitching on Jesse's boots. "Just give me a hand up, will you?" His hand found mine before I finished my sentence. "Having a stomach the size of Tibet has a way of tipping a person off balance."

When my eyes met his, I knew he saw through me, and he knew I knew. He knew I was trying to protect him as much as he was trying to protect me. The tricky part for me was that I had to keep my emotions veiled in order to protect him. He had the luxury of letting them go full tilt, which he took advantage of. Frequently.

Hiding my emotions might have been a skill of mine that a ninja would have admired a few years earlier, but I'd lost my edge since meeting Jesse. It was kind of like prying open a clam. Once they'd been broken open, you could try to close the pieces back together, but it was just an appearance. To look inside, all you had to do was lift the top. I thought Jesse knew that, and I loved him all the more for not taking the easy way and just sticking his head inside my closed curtains and looking to see what I was really feeling.

When I was standing beside him, he wrapped his other arm around my waist to steady me should I need it. His eyes were thick with worry, so I concentrated on draining mine of all traces of concern before I let him meet my gaze.

"Are you sure you're okay?" he asked again, his eyes running down the length of me before returning to mine.

I felt it again—a brief wave of dizziness right before my vision blurred. It passed almost as quickly as it came on though. I nodded and put on a convincing smile. "I'm okay." My voice sounded strong, just as I'd intended. "Are you okay?"

Jesse swallowed, his throat bobbing as he studied me with heavy eyes. "I'm okay," he said in the same tone. It was strong, but the kind of strong that was only conjured up to hide what we were really feeling. Scared. Helpless. Weak.

Neither of us would be "okay" until we made it through the next three months. Until we *all* made it through the next three months.

CHAPTER three

Rowen

TRAVELING THREE HUNDRED fifty miles in one day as a pregnant woman was not what I'd consider an ideal situation. Traveling those hundreds of miles while six month pregnant in *Old Bessie* . . . fell even a few rungs lower on the ideal ladder. The suspension wasn't bad, but the seats . . . they didn't recline or decline or any'cline at all. I'd learned to get really creative with a pillow, but each trip got worse. I'd breathe a few sighs of relief once we'd made our temporary move out here in the next couple of weeks and the next time I traveled an endless stretch of I-90 would be sans baby in my stomach.

My doctor appointment had run extra late, so by the time we made it into Missoula, Garth and Josie's engagement party had already started. After a quick stopover at Willow Springs to unload the luggage and change into clothes less wrinkled from travel and stained with drive-thru Mexican food, we were back in Old Bessie and cruising toward Garth and Josie's farmhouse, where the festivities were already well under way.

The drive to their place was only about twenty minutes, but I'd reached my upper limits of travel via ancient truck one hundred miles ago. I couldn't stop shifting and wiggling, trying to get comfortable. It was about as futile an endeavor as my efforts to disguise the small planet projecting from my stomach.

"Black, you were a loyal friend in the truest of ways." I ran my hands down the dark shift dress I'd slipped into. Instead of making my tummy look less out-there, it succeeded at the opposite. "You betray me in my darkest hour. I thought we were more than that."

Jesse chuckled and turned down the volume on Cash crooning through the cab. "What are you talking about? You look amazing."

Keeping one eye on the road, he managed to inspect me with the other in a way that made my throat run dry. I wasn't sure if that urge swelling inside me was more due to my hormones, that glimmer in his eye, or how he looked. It was probably some deadly combination of all three that was making my fists ball at my sides when they wanted to be ravaging my insanely hot husband. Teenage boys had nothing on pregnant women when it came to thinking about sex every two seconds. Nothing on us.

"What? I mean it," Jesse continued when he guessed I wasn't buying his "you look amazing" compliment. "How could you come out looking like that after ten minutes when I can barely manage to get my other boot on in the same amount of time?"

I smiled at him still checking me out like my stomach wasn't about to pop. He was convincing me, more with his face than his words, and really, I'd take any compliment anyone wanted to throw me these days. I wasn't picky.

"I was trained in the ways of the Jedi, that's how." I gave up trying to pull and stretch my dress to tone down my stomach because that just wasn't going to happen. The upside to my selection was that the material was light, which meant I'd stay cool when the dancing and music got crazy later on, as I knew it would with Garth and Josie at the party helm, and the neckline was cut low enough to just hint at my expanding chest. Maybe that would distract people from my stomach. It seemed to be working with my husband at least.

"How are you doing over there?" he asked when I shifted for the who-knows-how-many'th time. That glimmer dimmed from his eyes as I continued to adjust, and he helped me slide the pillow behind my lower back in an attempt to get comfortable.

"I'm doing so fabulous over here I can't sit still." I drew my leg up behind my lap and, surprisingly, found a comfortable position that way. In two minutes I'd be in agony again, but for right now, it was working.

"That's it. I can't do this again." Jesse thumped the steering wheel with his palm as he made the turn to Garth and Josie's. "We're buying a new car before we leave. I won't let you make another trip being so uncomfortable."

He'd been saying that since month four, when the fidgeting and squirming started, and I'd managed to steer him away from the idea with reassurances that I was okay, that it wasn't that bad, that I just needed to get out and stretch. After this trip though? I was close to agreeing with him.

I was just about to reply that maybe we could check out a few dealerships in town when I felt another one. A small, sharp exhale escaped my mouth as my arms wound around my stomach. I wasn't sure what they were, but it felt as if someone had wrapped a thick rubber band around my stomach, stretched it out, then let it snap back into place. The sensation was sharp and sudden, and that one seemed to be more persistent that the ones I'd started feeling after downing my third taquito outside of Spokane. I hadn't mentioned anything to Jesse about it because he probably would have whipped the truck around and sped right back to my doctor's office, and that seemed like a lot of effort for something that was likely indigestion.

This one, though . . . this one felt as though there might have been more at work than just indigestion. Probably gas. I tried to shake it off, but Jesse wouldn't let it go quite so easily.

"What's the matter?" He parked Old Bessie at the front of a line of cars and twisted in his seat after cutting the engine.

"Too many taquitos." I thumped my chest with my fist and tried to work up a burp to make it convincing. Of course when I really needed one, nada, but they sure didn't mind plaguing me the minute I laid my head down at night.

"Rowen, I know that eyebrow twitch. Something's wrong." Jesse's thumb tapped the center of my eyebrow, where I guessed the eyebrow was giving me away.

"The only something that's wrong is that I really want to throw myself on your lap and ravage you until you're a cross-eyed, stuttering mess, but that's become a physical impossibility." My hand patted my stomach. There was no way I could fit on his lap in my condition unless I wanted to wear a steering wheel dent in my back for the next couple of days.

"Rowen—"

"Yeah, yeah, I know. The doctor says I shouldn't do

anything that would tax my heart too much, which you interpret to be anything and everything from lifting a fork to getting it on like Donkey Kong with my husband." I unbuckled and reached for the door handle because I'd been de-nied so many times I didn't know why I kept trying. Jesse would give me anything . . . as long as he wasn't under the impression it would threaten my life.

"Hey, don't go. You know I want to. I would if we could." His hand dropped to my thigh as he scooted closer. "We just . . . can't."

I think it was the hand draped across my leg that triggered level two of my advance. Not that it would be any more successful than the last one, but I was a slow learner. And persistent if nothing else. "We can't because it will make my heart rate amp up, which in your warped head translates to it going off like a grenade inside of my chest, which would mean you'd have to spend the rest of your life without me which, I agree, is a tragedy if there ever was one."

He was smiling. That was a good thing. Jesse didn't smile as much as he used to. He still smiled more than the average person, but his smile-to-frown ratio had been drastically affected.

"But what if I could keep my heartbeat nice and steady, a solid eighty beats a minute?" I asked.

He gave me a look that said he knew better. He was right. But just because I'd never been able to do *that* without achieving heart rate records didn't mean I couldn't. I'd just never had the proper motivation to try to keep it low. I had the proper motivation now.

"Well?" I pressed when he stayed quiet.

"Well nothing. What you're suggesting . . ." His head

shook. "It's impossible."

"Improbable maybe. But not impossible."

"You"—his hand squeezed my leg—"you're insane."

"And you're about to join me if you abstain for another three months. All of that *abstaining*"—I cleared my throat as my eyes darted to his lap—"is like poison to your body. In your efforts to save my life, you can't let yours be threatened."

I scooted closer to him, my hopes just starting to lift, when he reached across me and threw open the door. Nothing like a flood of fresh air and getting denied—*again*—to clear a girl's head.

"That's just plain mean," I grumbled as I climbed out of the cab, Jesse holding one of my hands so I didn't take a spill. Center of gravity—totally thrown off now.

Jesse crawled out behind me. "Need me to grab anything?"

"I need you to grab lots of things," I muttered, adjusting my dress because *hello!* I was going for demure cleavage, not porn-star cleavage. "But why don't you grab Garth and Josie's engagement present from the bed right now, and I'll try working on those other things later?"

He leaned over the side of the truck to grab their present. I took no shame in checking out his backside and wondering if I'd ever be able to sculpt that level of perfection. Probably not.

"I'm not budging on this." His voice was light and easy, but I knew the weight of his words.

"Good. I'm not budging on my personal agenda either." I crossed my arms. "And we both know who's more cunning and holds more championships in the sex department, Jesse, because look at what I'm holding." I raised my hand, my fingers pinched together as if I were holding something in the air. "Your V card. I wanted it, and it's mine. I wanted to marry you, and you're mine." I kept his imaginary V card in the air, ignoring his eye roll, and stole a few steps closer. "I want you, here and now."

His jaw tightened, along with his hands that curled tighter around the retrieved present.

"And I'll have you somewhere around here, sometime around now." I circled my finger around our surroundings and let my gaze penetrate his until I knew my message had been received. I was past tired of this abstinence game. My heart was a little twitchy, not some trap about to be sprung. The doctor had advised against all sorts of "vigorous" activities, and while that might have been the ideal way to enjoy intimacy, it didn't have to be the only way. The whole "beggars can't be choosers" things was especially relevant at this impasse in my life.

His shoulders rose and fell from his sigh. "I love you, Rowen." He kissed my temple before starting for the barn, where the party was in full swing from the sounds of it. "But no."

I watched him walk away, admiring him when I should have been glaring at him from his continued denial. It would be easier to endure the no-sex policy if I wasn't married to quite possibly the sexiest man in existence. "I love you too, Jesse," I said to myself, starting toward him when he stopped to wait for me. "But yes."

When I made my way to him and he looped an arm around my waist while managing to balance the present with his other hand, I made myself drop the subject. For now. The harder I pushed my side, the harder he pushed his, so I'd just have to come at it from a different angle.

One he wouldn't expect and one he hopefully wouldn't see coming until I had him on his back and clothing free.

"Is this an engagement party or a bachelor party?" I said as we closed in on the barn.

"Knowing those two, it's probably both."

Garth had moved into the old farmhouse so he could keep fixing it up between work. Given his work included rodeoing and running a ranch, he hadn't gotten very far in the fix-up department, but it was still a nice enough place without all of the updates and finishing touches. The barn was a ways off from the house, and it was giant. It was almost as large as the barn at Willow Springs, and compared to the modest farmhouse it shared a plot of land with, the barn seemed to overwhelm the entire area. With the country music blaring from it, seeming to shake its foundation, along with the shouts within, the barn only further defined the land.

The large double doors were propped open, allowing a steady stream of people to flow in and out of party headquarters.

"Whoa," was all I could say when we stepped inside.

The barn had been transformed into something pulled from *Country Living* magazine. There were still cowboys drinking and spitting and heckling each other, and there were still herds of kids running around the place like it was a playground, and there were remnants of hay still dotting the old wood floor, but Josie and her mom had clearly taken the reins with the decorations, and they'd outdone themselves.

An endless web of white lights were strung above, weaving around the rafters and beams like they had too many lights and too few places to wrap them. The place was awash with the gentle glow streaming down. White lanterns hung from long silk ribbons, high enough to be out of the way but low enough a person could almost reach up and touch them. Staggered around the outer edges were bales of hay with the same ivory silk ribbon tied around them, complete with a cardboard heart with G & J hanging off the bow.

It was country chic at its finest.

And that was when I heard the hooting and hollering from the back corner. Okay, so it was country chic plus a mechanical bull.

So Garth had been allowed his two cents in the décor department.

"I'm going to drop this off at the gift table, then you're slow, *slow* dancing with me." Jesse eyed the dance floor while backing up toward the gift table.

That was appealing on just about every level except . . . "Maybe we should, you know, say hey to the bride-and groom-to-be first? Following up the saying hey trend to your family too?" I eyed the dance floor, wondering what I was saying. There were few things I enjoyed more than dancing with Jesse. Especially when he gathered me against him like he was trying to protect me from the whole world at the same time he was ready to take it on with me.

After carefully propping the wrapped engagement gift up against the table, he grabbed my hand and led me across the barn. We were both thinking the same thing. If the happily engaged couple weren't whooping it up somewhere around that mechanical bull, then the world had shifted off its axis.

The barn was packed. There were so many bodies

dancing, talking, and hollering around it that I was immensely thankful I'd slipped into something light and breathable. Jesse was in a nice button-down shirt and was already reaching for the cuffs to roll them up.

"Do you see your family anywhere?" I didn't quite have to shout, but close.

Jesse's head shook. "But no doubt they've seen us. Or at least my mom has. You could be on the opposite side of the county and she could still zero in on you. It's that grandmother telepathy or something."

A chuckle slipped past my lips. "The same county? Come on. Give her more credit than that. Try the same *country*."

Jesse's laugh tangled with mine as we moved toward the bucking bull in the back. I'd just seen some guy get tossed from it so violently he looked like a flying squirrel jettisoning through the air.

"I can't believe Garth managed to convince Josie to throw a mechanical bull into the mix. Classy"—I waved at the jaw-dropping scene we'd been welcomed with before flashing my hand in front of us—where someone else was throwing his leg over the back of the bull—"meet trashy. Get acquainted with one another because something tells me you're going to be seeing a lot of each other around these parts."

Jesse grinned at the ground as we weaved through the crowd, and I focused on the guy who'd just thrown himself onto the bull. There were plenty of black hats dotted around the barn, but that one stood out for some reason. Maybe because that hat demanded to be noticed as much as its owner did.

"Get that rookie off that thing before he hurts himself!" Jesse cupped his hand around his mouth and hollered at Garth, who was shifting around on the back of the bull, trying to find his sweet spot like tens of thousands of dollars were on the line.

"Yeah!" I joined in, my voice not carrying nearly as far as Jesse's. "Before he busts his back or something!"

Jesse whistled quietly, his forehead creasing as he looked at me. "That was low."

"Oh, please. He didn't even hear it." I waved at Garth, who was probably still trying to find that damn sweet spot, but a quick look at him revealed he was looking our way. Well, he was looking *my* way.

"I heard that, Sterling-Walker!" he shouted. "And I'd say something real colorful in reply if it wasn't for that little papoose in your stomach that Jesse's convinced can hear every last foul word I say." Garth tipped his hat in our direction, firing a wink. "Nice of you two to make it, by the way. Hope our little engagement party didn't throw a wrench in you city slickers' social calendars."

I stepped up to the edge of the bull pit until my knees bumped into the mats. "Are you going to ride that bull sometime tonight? Or keep running your mouth?"

Another wink. "I'm not just going to ride this bull, Sterling-Walker. I'm going to make it my bitch."

"Black!" Jesse hollered as he shouldered up beside me. "Language!"

Garth snapped his fingers as he made a face. "Fuck, I forgot."

"Really?" Jesse flagged his arms at my stomach.

"What can I say, Jess? I'm a foul-mouthed bastard." Garth's dark eyes were flashing. He was clearly enjoying himself. Talking trash on the back of a bull . . . yeah, that was pretty much the inner circle of heaven for a guy like him.

"And that's three," Jesse said before lunging onto the mats and charging Garth and the bull.

Garth didn't stand a chance, not with the way Jesse was hauling. Not to mention he'd just been distracted by Josie sauntering up to the edge of the pit and gracing him with a look that should have been strictly reserved for the bedroom. Garth didn't notice Jesse until he was launching through the air at Garth, but by then, no matter how settled into his sweet spot he was, Garth wasn't staying on the back of that bull.

When Jesse crashed into Garth, they both tumbled over the side of the bull, landed on the mats with a loud *thunk*, and that was the end of it.

"Don't cuss in front of my kid, Black." Jesse propped up on his elbows and looked at him.

Garth was reaching for his hat to slide it back on, but Jesse's had tumbled over the side of the mat. "Don't show up to my next engagement party an hour late," Garth threw back as if he was all kinds of put out, but the two of them still shook hands and wound up cracking smiles.

"Deal. Because next time my wife won't be pregnant, so we won't have to spend an hour camped out in a waiting room before enduring another nail-biting ultrasound before having to wait another hour for the doctor to actually show up in the exam room."

My hands flew to my hips at almost the precise moment Josie's snapped to hers.

She got the first words in. "Excuse me? Your *next* engagement party? Who exactly are you planning on getting engaged to next?"

Jesse swatted Garth's arm. Garth swatted right back before rolling onto his side and giving Josie a look that I knew would melt her defenses. "Come on now, Joze. You know what I meant. The jealous woman act doesn't become you, babe."

Josie crossed her arms tighter, but her face was smoothing out. "Oh yeah? Why not?"

A crowd was gathered around the bull pit, but the two of them were acting as if they were only two in the vast barn.

"Because to be jealous, you have to feel some sort of inclination that your man could be lured away by someone else, right?" Garth covered the spot above his heart with his hands. "But, baby, you know the only girl for me is the one I'm staring at right now."

Josie's arms unfolded, and what was left of the creases lining her face melted. I didn't know how anyone could look at Garth Black like he was God in human form, but it was an expression Josie had frequently.

"You're forgiven," she hollered at him. "Just watch who you talk about second engagements around, will ya? Next time you'll be punished accordingly." The hints of a smile pulled at Josie's mouth.

"*That,* Joze, does not sound like a threat. But understood."

I didn't know if Garth had blinked since their conversation-meets-lovers'-quarrel had started, but that was normal. It was like he took a blinking hiatus when Josie was around, as if he didn't want to waste a moment viewing the dark side of his eyelids when she was in front of him.

Josie still hadn't seen me—I wasn't sure she'd noticed Jesse out there beside Garth—but I wasn't going to distract her from whatever moment she and Garth were sharing. Because fiancés falling off bulls after being tackled before rambling about second engagements in the middle of an ancient barn was the very pinnacle of romance. But based on the way she was still staring at her husband-to-be, that was the pinnacle for Josie. I couldn't decide how I felt about that, but I didn't need to decide how *I* felt about it. It was as clear as the bump projecting from my abdomen that *she* was happy.

When Jesse crawled my way like he was a soldier shimmying under barbed wire, a goofy grin on his face, I felt my crossed arms start to give up. It took a lot of energy either pretending to be or actually being upset at someone, and I didn't have an excess of energy lately, most of all tonight. This whole day, I felt like something had found my energy switch and flipped it off. I couldn't find a way to switch it back.

"Have I mentioned how grateful I am that you're not as touchy as most women?" Jesse said when he made it to the edge of the mat in front of me.

"Not following," I said as someone hurled his hat across the mechanical bull at him. Instead of landing closer to him, it landed almost directly on my head. I grabbed the hat before it tumbled to the floor, and I dropped it on my head and waited.

Jesse's smile grew when he studied me in his hat. "You know. Some women, they're like grenades. With the slightest of mishaps, they can tear apart half a city block."

I had to bite the inside of my mouth to keep from smiling. "Garth Black, stop channeling him. I like my Jesse Walker only about infinitely more."

Dropping my hand to his head, I mussed his crown of

thick, light hair that spent way too much time hidden under a hat. Jesse had the kind of hair women would die for and male models would kill for. Part of me kind of liked that few people saw him without his hat though. The top of his head and hair were a secret I was one of the few people in on. I liked having parts of him I didn't have to share with the world. That was what made a relationship special—that a person knew the secrets and parts of someone they kept hidden from the rest of the world, and stood shoulder to shoulder with them no matter what.

"All I'm saying is that I'm thankful you don't get riled up and ticked off every time I say something wrong or do something not quite how I should have. It's nice to go through life on solid ground instead of quicksand and glass." Jesse swung his legs over the side of the mats and sat on the edge, looking at me with eyes so light, it didn't seem possible the world around us was dark.

"You've said so few wrong things and done so few wrong things in your life that the verdict is still out as to if you're human . . . but you're welcome. Nice to know my lack of drama is appreciated." I let him pull me closer when his arms wound around my waist. "However, I'm not sure I can let what you just said out there go."

Jesse's head tipped. To him, it was already forgotten, but to me, I wasn't so sure I could forget it.

"About me not being pregnant next time," I said, jump-starting his memory. "I didn't realize you'd made that decision for us. Or felt it was your duty to decide for us."

His eyes closed for a moment as a sigh escaped his mouth. I'd heard him mention before that one pregnancy was enough for him, but I'd thought that was the stressed-to-the-max version of him grasping at whatever strings of perceived control he could. Just now though, he hadn't been an anxiety-ridden wreck. He'd been as relaxed as I'd seen him in weeks.

"I'm sorry it came out that way. You're right. It did sound like I'd made some executive decision I hadn't gone over with you first." He rubbed the back of his neck, staring across the barn as if he were hoping the right words would paint themselves across the walls. "I just figured, you know, after all we've been through with this one . . . it would be our last." His eyes flitted to my stomach, lingering for a moment, before returning to the barn.

"If we have any more kids, it won't go like this. You realize that, right? If we want to have another, I'll get the surgery, and the next one will be a breeze. You won't have to worry about me fainting from a walk in the park or passing out if I want to vacuum the carpet or my heart saying *sayonara* at the drop of a hat. The next one would be entirely different." I was hot, tired, emotional, and that snapping/squeezing sensation was still making me its personal project, so I should have been the one hell-bent on never doing this again. Why was I the one making the argument for more babies? I hadn't made it through this one yet.

Jesse's hand slid around my back, pausing on the swell of my stomach. I'd swear from the look on his face as he switched between staring at my belly and my face, it was as if he was deciding which to save and which to let go of. Agony and guilt swam in my husband's eyes, and I was used to the opposite. That was why I found myself worrying about him making it through this twice as much as I worried about me making it through.

"Right now, Rowen, I just can't even consider doing this again. This one's been hard enough, you know?" His voice was so quiet, he could have been talking to himself, but I heard every word. "Once we make it through this, we can talk about doing it again, but right now, this is all I can handle. I'm sorry if that makes me weak, but that's how I feel. I can't pretend I don't."

My frustration melted, leaving in its place something not quite so fiery hot, but something that brought a slow, rolling warmth. It felt a lot like comfort.

"That doesn't make you weak. That makes you strong." I stole the remaining space between us and dropped my hands around the back of his neck, lacing my fingers together. "If you were weak, you'd find a way to weed out some of the feelings you have for me and this baby. If you were weak, you'd be looking for any and every possible way to ease your pain instead of accepting it and focusing on lessening mine. If you were weak, you'd find some way to care less so if something did happen, it wouldn't bowl you over, just make you stumble back a few steps." If I could have crawled into his lap and kissed the worry out of him, I would have, but Jesse's ran too deep for me to remove. The only thing that could free him wouldn't come for another few months. "To be strong, you have to know your weaknesses, confront them, and ultimately accept them. A person isn't strong because they lack weakness but because they don't let it guide them."

He swallowed like he was trying to clear a tennis ball lodged in his throat, then he pulled me closer and dropped his head carefully to the swell of my stomach. His forehead still creased, his eyes closed as I ran my fingers through his hair. Every few strokes, another crease would unfold until a minute later, Jesse had either found a sliver of peace or fallen asleep with my stomach as a pillow.

I let him stay like that, not wanting to disturb him in a rare moment of solitude, continuing to comb my fingers through his hair in the way I imagined I'd calm our child one day. I was so used to Jesse being a beacon of strength, it was a relief when I caught a glimpse of just how human he was.

It seemed like an entire night had passed when in fact probably only a few minutes had, but I was brought back to reality when the same black-hat-sporting cowboy leapt onto the same bull he'd just been tackled off of. From the shade and sparkle of his lips, he'd been tackled by someone else too.

"Get out your composition books and take notes, people," Garth shouted into the crowd gathering around the pit now that Mr. Championship Buckle was going to give them a show. "Because you're about to witness how a real cowboy doesn't just ride a bull but stays on one."

Jesse remained in his temporary hypnosis, but I smirked at Garth, whose normally bloated ego had reached new heights. From the corner of my eyes, I noticed Josie kick off her boots and bound across the wide circle of mats toward the bull and Ego-rific. In one insanely graceful move I'd be lucky to manage on my least-pregnant day, Josie leapt onto the bull behind Garth. She cinched her arms tightly around him as she pressed her lap as far into his ass as it would go.

In under five seconds, I caught no fewer than three emotions filter through Garth's eye. Surprise, to excitement, to a different kind of excitement when Josie's chest pressed into his back.

"I'm more of a learn-through-doing type of girl than by watching," Josie said with a smile so evil the devil could have been taking his own notes.

"One rider only!" the guy standing by the controls and wearing a shirt that read A-Z Rentals shouted.

Josie didn't have a chance to pout before Garth glanced at the guy. "I'll pay you an extra hundred to 'overlook' that rule this once."

The guy's lips clamped together and stayed that way, his hand moving to the control panel.

Josie stuck her head over Garth's shoulder. "I thought we were saving for a honeymoon?"

"Baby, this right here is a honeymoon." He shifted on the bull, although it had less to do with adjusting himself into the sweet spot and more about adjusting up on Josie. When she leaned closer and whispered something in his ear, his brows disappeared into his hat. "Now this is the way God intended man to ride bull. With a sexy-ass woman straddling him from behind mouthing filthy things into his ear."

I rolled my eyes at the two of them doing their thing, but really, it was pretty damn amazing. Garth and Josie's love story was almost as unconventional and unlikely as Jesse's and mine.

"Hang on, Josie!" someone hollered at her as the bull started to move.

"Josie's an old pro at this," Garth hollered back, clamping one hand over Josie's hands around his chest, the other holding onto the bull. "She's had plenty of experience riding beasts of an imposing, well-hung, might I add, nature."

I didn't miss Garth scanning the room before letting

that comment fly. Those two might have been engaged, but I didn't doubt Mr. Gibson wouldn't hesitate to rip Garth apart, appendage by appendage, if he heard Garth mention his daughter's experience riding well-endowed animals.

"Well-hung's a matter of perspective, Black!" Someone chortled in the crowd as Garth and Josie moved a bit faster on the bull.

Garth found whoever it was in the crowd and lifted a dark brow. "I don't know. Your girl's 'perspective' on that matter didn't leave any room for disappointment."

A chorus of "ooooohs" circled the pit as the bull spun and moved in an almost lazy loll.

"Come on, I ain't no grandma whose had both hips and a knee replaced. Stop insulting me and give me a ride here," Garth called to the guy at the controls, who was fighting a smile at Garth Black riding a mechanical bull in granny mode. His wasn't the only smile floating around the pit. "Make it hard, for Christ's sakes."

That was when Josie's hand slid down his chest, lingered just above his belt buckle, and wound down his thigh. It was a little too inner thigh for this public of a setting in my opinion, but Josie had never let someone else's opinion get in the way of what she wanted or didn't want. She had Garth's attention from about the belt buckle point, and when she angled her head closer toward his, Garth's whole face changed from being in control of a situation to having none in a different one. That man was so hopeless when it came to her that she could have only been using him to harvest his internal organs and he wouldn't have cared.

When she moved closer, her eyes dropping to his

mouth, he followed the cue, and tipping his hat back just enough, Garth lowered his mouth to Josie's. There they were, making out up on top of a mechanical bull in front of a barn full of family and friends. It was what I loved about them. They made fairy tales a reality in a very public way, where Jesse and I preferred to keep our own tale more private.

The bull took a very sudden and sharp jolt, which was promptly followed by the newly engaged couple flying off the back of it before thumping into the mats. The crowd around the bull erupted in shouts and claps, but not even that could break Jesse from his stupor. I was glad. Peaceful moments were so rare for him, I'd started to wonder if he was capable of recreating them. After firing a glare at the guy chuckling at the controls, Garth pulled Josie up and headed toward us.

"Nice ride there, Black. Plenty of noteworthy material I can apply in 'How *Not* to Ride a Bull.'" I waved at Josie, who was covering her mouth as though she'd just noticed we were here.

Garth tried to fire a scowl at me as he adjusted his hat, but his eyes gave him away. He was happy. So much so, I doubted if anything could strip him of it.

"I'm so glad you guys were able to make it." The moment Josie crawled off of the mats, her hands dropped to my stomach, spaced around Jesse, who was snapping out of his temporary hypnosis. Josie had always been a hugger, but after I'd started to show, she became one of those pregnant-stomach touchers too. It was like a baby inside a belly was a magnet she couldn't resist the pull of. "What a nightmare with all of the waiting you guys had today. Didn't those doctors know you guys had a party to get to tonight?"

Jesse lifted his head from my stomach, more because Josie's hands were invading his space than him looking like he wanted to. "Sorry we're late." He sounded tired, his voice thick like when he woke up in the morning. "But happy we're here now." He managed a smile for Josie before holding his hand out to shake Garth's.

"See? I told you they'd make it. You can relax now and enjoy the rest of the night." Josie glanced at Garth before getting back to staring at my stomach as she massaged little circles into it.

It kinda freaked me out, and I would have put a hard stop to it if it was anyone but Josie, but she had always been one of those touchy-feely types. Her running her hands all over me was like someone else nodding at me in acknowledgement.

"Yeah, yeah. They made it. You were right," Garth replied, his lips still shiny and sparkly from Josie's lip gloss.

"This guy's been pouting half the night, worrying you two wouldn't make it in time," Josie said, waving at someone who offered a congrats in passing. "He said the only people who are his real friends wouldn't make it and he'd be stuck making nice with everyone else who was only here because of me." Josie circled her finger around the barn brimming with people. "Because, you know, the world is out to get and totally against Garth Black."

"This might be a bad time to bring this up, but the only reason Jesse and I are here is because of Josie too."

Garth gave me a tight smile as a beer magically appeared over his shoulder. So much for no friends in the crowd.

"Why doesn't this man have a cold beer in his hands yet?" Garth motioned at Jesse, who'd just shoved off of the mats to take his sentinel at my side. Answering his own question, he held his beer out for Jesse.

Jesse didn't seem to notice it. Instead he looked like he was still trying to wake up and figure out where he was.

Garth grabbed Jesse's hand, opened it, and slipped the beer in. "There you go, Jess. Now it's a party."

I didn't know if it was the condensation dripping down the side of the bottle into his hand or if he'd just figured out a way to push the last of the fog aside, but Jesse's eyes cleared. After taking a look at the three of us, he glanced at the beer. "It's your party. You need this more than I do." He lifted the beer toward Garth, who shook his head as adamantly as I'd ever seen him.

"No. You most definitely need that more than I do," he said, waving when Jesse tried to hand it off again. "Besides, I've already met my two-beer limit for the night, so I'm going to pretend to be a good boy and refrain from all bottles unless there's water inside." Garth lifted his chin at the people around us. "Half of these people are only here for the free food and the hope I'll demonstrate just how much of Clay Black is inside these veins. You know how much I love disappointing people. It's one of the few things I do really well." Garth winked at me then kissed Josie's cheek before backing into the crowd. "Speaking of bottles of zero-proof liquid, you want me to grab you one, mama bear?"

Jesse nodded for me while I shook my own head. I'd been drinking so much water today, yesterday, and every day since two pink lines drove a wrecking ball through our lives, I'd actually checked the internet to see how much a person had to drink before it became a bad thing. That was another thing my husband was ever on the ball on—keeping a water bottle within reach and topped off.

"Okay, so do I grab one or don't I?" Garth waved his finger between Jesse and me.

"Yes."

"No," I said at the same time.

Both of us followed it up with a sigh.

"It's hot in here. You need to stay cool, hydrated," Jesse said, glancing at my forehead where I could feel sweat beading. "It can't hurt."

Instead of arguing, I turned it into a negotiation. "Fine. I'll drink a bottle of water." His face ironed out in surprise, probably because I never gave in so quickly or easily. "*If* you drink that bottle of beer."

His face pinched back together. "What does me drinking a beer have to do with you drinking water?"

"Nothing." I lifted a shoulder. "And everything."

"Shit, you guys. This can't be that difficult of a decision." From his tone, I could imagine the impatient look on Garth's face.

Jesse threw him a quick glare for "defiling" our innocent baby's ears before aiming his attention back at me. "This is crazy."

"I know." I lifted his hand holding the beer toward his mouth. "Isn't it great?"

With a disgruntled sigh, he lifted the bottle to his lips and took a sip.

"That's fine. You want to nurse your bottle all night long? I will too." I waved Garth on his water-retrieving way but crossed my arms at Jesse.

"So are you implying that for every bottle of beer I

drink, you'll drink your own bottle of water?" He took another sip, this one not so dainty.

"I didn't realize I was implying anything. I thought it was pretty obvious."

"You're bribing me."

Yeah, I kinda was. "I'm trying to get you to loosen up for one night and have a good time."

Finally done running her hands all over my stomach, Josie held her fist out for me. I bumped mine against hers.

"Unbelievable," Jesse muttered, taking another even longer drink of his beer.

I smiled. He hadn't had a single drink since he'd found out I was pregnant. When most men would have been reaching for the bottle, Jesse's got shoved to the back of the fridge. I figured that with his low tolerance even before three months without alcohol, he'd be putty in my hungry, very horny, hands after three, possibly four beers.

Better make it five just to be safe. I wanted him good and tipsy so all I had to do was crook my finger to get him to come running, but I didn't want him drunk and sloppy. After my own three-month stint of going without, I wanted to take my time and do it right. More than once if possible.

By the time Garth had returned with a few waters, Jesse had almost downed his whole bottle. Sloshing what was left of it in front of me, he lifted an expectant brow at the bottle in my hands.

Two could so easily play at this game.

After unscrewing the lid, I clinked my bottle to his and lifted it to my mouth while I heard Josie whisper to Garth what was going on. Another curse flooded from his mouth. I took my own dainty sip at first, and just when Jesse was crossing his arms, I tipped the bottle back and drained all sixteen ounces in the time it took Garth to mutter yet another comment that would earn his forehead a dent the size of Jesse's fist if he didn't watch it.

"Well?" I waved the empty bottle in Jesse's face. His eyes were wide with surprise. "What's it going to be? Your wife's and child's well-being, hydration included, is in your hands."

Jesse's head fell some, his eyes drifting to my stomach. When he looked up, I saw a look of resolve I was all too familiar with.

"Black," he called, his voice matching his expression, "get me another."

CHAPTER four

Jesse

MY HEAD WAS swimming, and my body was floating. I couldn't remember how many beers I'd had, but it hadn't been many. At least too few to feel so hazed. Given my low tolerance to all things of an alcoholic nature paired with the added clincher of not having had a single drink for the past few months, the three or four or five I'd had the past couple of hours was screwing with me like I was a teen girl who'd just busted into her parents' liquor cabinet and reached for a bottle of peach schnapps.

I wasn't quite drunk, but I was close enough to realize I needed to cut myself off unless I want Garth to have to peel me off of the barn floor. Rowen had kept up with our agreement . . . bet . . . *thing*, matching my every bottle of beer for her own bottle of water. So that meant she'd had three or four or five too, which should be more than enough.

Except it was so hot in the barn it felt as if my skin was about to start peeling off. Garth had opened up the back barn doors when the heat hit stifling levels, but of course it would be the night when not even the faintest of summer breezes would grace us with its presence. So it was hot. Ungodly hot. Rowen was wearing something light which *should* keep her cool, but her arms and chest had been coated with a sheen of sweat for the past hour. She was seeping water as quickly as she could drink it.

Not to mention she'd hardly drank anything on the drive over because she had complained that if she downed more than a thimble of water an hour, she had to hit every rest stop and gas station we passed. A pregnant woman needed at least three liters of fluid every day, so given that each bottle was . . . I squinted in an attempt to focus on the miniscule numbers stamped on her water bottle . . . okay, the first number was definitely a one, but the second one could be a six . . . it could just as easily be an eight.

I gave my head a swift shake to see if that would help clear my vision, but it seemed to do the opposite. So it was either sixteen or eighteen ounces. If she'd had three or four or five—let's say four as a safe average—that meant she'd had about . . .

Math's hard. That was all I could think as I made my third attempt to multiply four by sixteen, then eighteen. I couldn't arrive at the right answer, but I arrived at a conclusion. She hadn't had her daily recommended value of fluid.

I'd reached mine, beer-wise, after I lifted my second bottle to my lips, but I was a big guy—my body could take it. Rowen's though? Hers was too fragile to risk chancing something as important as hydration.

"Is that another empty bottle I see you clutching?" Rowen's arm wound around my back as she nestled into my chest. "I'll flag someone to bring you another."

I had to shake the bottle in my hand. Nothing. When

she cocked an eyebrow, I lowered my gaze to the water bottle she was holding.

"Mine's empty," I said, resting my hand on her back. Even through the thin layer of her dress, I could feel her sweat. I felt that familiar sensation cinching around my stomach, almost like an invisible vise had been attached and was being clamped down. It had been getting worse and more frequent, triggered now by something as simple as Rowen sweating a little. My neurotic switch might have been triggered from the moment she'd flashed those two pink lines in my face, but I hadn't started out like this. No, my fall into hard-core *loco* had been a daily regressive effort. "Yours is not."

Rowen's hand moved lower down my back, her thumb curling through a belt loop and giving it a few tugs. "This is fun." She smiled at me and tapped my nose, which was starting to tingle. "I like this game of You Drink, I Drink."

When she pressed closer to me, her fingers splaying more into ass than back territory, I felt something flicker to life that I'd been doing my damndest to repress. That flicker grew to a rolling flame when I saw the unsaid things in her eyes. Things that should stay unsaid in public but positively sighed, cried, or exhaled in private. That was the alcohol's fault too.

If it hadn't been for alcohol doing what it did best and lowering my inhibitions, I would have been able to drop a cage around that flicker then douse it in baking soda and aim a fire hose at it before it had the chance to ignite into something else.

I already knew what she wanted—she'd made no secret of it—and I knew she knew I wanted the same thing.

But I couldn't have that. Or I *wouldn't* let myself. Not until she and the baby were both given a clean bill of health and I could stop worrying about her heart giving out if I did so much as kiss her too hard.

"Yeah, but your part of this game can't make you upheave the contents of your stomach all over your boots, or whoever's boots are close by."

Rowen peeked down at her feet. She wasn't wearing boots like most everyone else was. Her feet had been swelling whenever she'd been on her feet or in the heat, and since she knew she'd be experiencing both tonight, she'd ditched the boots and thrown on a pair of sandals she could adjust as her ankles swelled into the night.

"No, but I spent the first four months of this pregnancy upheaving the contents of my stomach all over my boots, your boots, and every other surface within a ten-foot hurling radius." Her fingers curled into my backside, almost making me flinch. It seemed kind of weird to grope my ass after talking about puking, but I wasn't in a rush to complain. "I think you can suck it up for one night. Besides, you've just finished your fourth beer, and even though it should be an impossibility at your stature that you'd look as buzzed as you do, I think you'll survive another"—she tipped her head from side to side—"three or four more."

If I had one more, I'd be line dancing on the rafters. If I had three or four more, I'd be hungover into Sunday morning.

"Are you calling me a lightweight?" I asked, not really caring what she called me as long as she didn't stop touching and looking at me the way she was now.

She tapped my nose again. "I'm calling you a *feath-*

*er*weight, oh no-alcohol-tolerance husband of mine."

"You're right. I surrender." I lifted my hand clutching the empty beer bottle. "I'm a disgrace to my gender and my cowboy kind. So why don't we call this game on account of a touchy stomach? But first, you've got to finish your bottle like I finished mine."

Challenge was written on her face as she lifted the bottle to her mouth. Gripping the lid with her teeth, she unscrewed it all slow and deliberate like, her eyes trained on mine the entire time. Letting the lid fall from her lips, she caught it with one hand as she tipped the bottle to her mouth with the other. She didn't blink until she'd finished the water in one long drink.

Tossing it over her shoulder, she tipped her head at me, the challenge going another level deeper. "So what's it going to be, Walker? One more? Or no more?"

I swallowed, realizing the game she was playing and what she hoped to get if she was declared the victor. I also knew that after another beer or two, I'd have lost my ability to put up a fight. The last of my fraying inhibitions would be frazzled.

Like she was a mind reader and picking up on everything I was warring with, she ran her forearm across her forehead. "Wow. It sure is hot in here. I don't know about you, but I'm sweating like I'm six months pregnant and have just been chained inside a sauna."

"Then have some more water. Let's go cool off and get some fresh air." Those were obvious solutions to the hot problem, right? Go brainpower for not totally failing me.

"Sure, I'll have another bottle of water," she said with the nuance of *if only* in her tone. "If you have another beer."

"Rowen." I shook my head.

"Jesse." She nodded her head.

I held out another few seconds then gave up with an exasperated sigh. "Fine. But *one* more. And if you pull that same 'I'm hot and dehydrated' thing at the bottom of that bottle, I'm throwing you over my shoulder and dragging you outside before hooking you up to an H2O I.V."

Her mouth twitched. She knew as well as I did that she was twice as clever as me and double that in the cunning department. "Deal."

I didn't want to leave the warmth and welcome of her hold, but her water was empty, and if she was going to down another one, I had my own downing to do. "I'll be right back." I backed up in the direction of the beverage table but tripped over . . . my own two feet.

"You better be. I've got big plans for you tonight." Rowen fired a little wave at me as I cut through the crowd.

I knew exactly what her big plans were, but I wasn't going to step into her trap. Or I wasn't going to step into it any farther than I already had. No way.

The crowd had only grown larger and rowdier, but it wasn't like anyone was throwing fists (yet) or passing out drunk in the corners (yet). Everyone was having a good time—dancing, drinking, and eating—and from the looks of it, I was the only one going against the popular trend. It wasn't like I was incapable of enjoying Garth and Josie's engagement party under typical conditions, but nothing about the past few months had been "typical."

Even through the considerable fog of the beer, I was so worried about Rowen that it took priority above all else. A few guys slapped me on the back in passing, clinking their beers against my empty bottle, and I could tell my dad and mom were hoping to catch up with us some more by the way they kept glancing Rowen's and my way no matter who they were talking with, but I just wasn't in the mood for keeping up a conversation. After the long appointment and the long drive, what I was in the mood for was crawling into a warm bed beside my wife and falling asleep. Or at least, trying and pretending to be asleep.

My parents knew I was having a tough time and had done their best to offer support without suffocating me in it, but the tension of the unsaid was still suffocating in its own way. After stopping by to say hi and get the update on how the appointment had gone, Dad and Mom had given us both a big hug, said they'd see us at the house later on, and drifted into the party to find the older crowd so we could hang out with our younger crowd.

Other than Josie and Garth though, the only person I'd wanted to hang out with was Rowen. Our lives had been so busy that when we both had a night off, I didn't want to waste it catching up with a bunch of old friends. I wanted to spend it holding my wife and catching up a lot or a little with her. That would have been the case no matter what, but it had taken on a new significance ever since I'd learned what I could lose and how soon I could lose her.

I wasn't going to waste a second making small talk with some random acquaintance if I had my choice.

"Hey, Walker! I'm not used to seeing you make repeat trips to the bar. Must be having a rough night or a great one." Dustin, who ran one of the small bars in town, greeted me as I walked-slash-staggered toward him. Garth and Josie had hired him to bartend the party, and he was a classic bartender: good listener, better talker.

"I'm having a bit of both," I answered, praying he wouldn't feel the need to offer another lecture on parenting as he had when I'd swung by for my last beer. Somehow I wasn't grasping the concept of how good cop/bad cop worked with infants.

"Same thing as before? Beer and a water? Or do you want me to liven up your night a bit more than that water marinated in hops and barley can do?" Dustin made a few clucking sounds as he reached for something I wouldn't chance inhaling, let alone ingesting.

"Believe me, my life is so livened up, I can barely handle it." I nodded at the beers and grabbed two waters from one of the giant metal buckets on the table. If for every drink of beer, I took one of water, I could mitigate my getting drunker chances.

Dustin waited a minute, like he was waiting for me to change my mind, before pulling a beer out of the ice and popping off the cap. "You know where to find me when you need something harder than three proof." He handed the icy bottle to me with another cluck.

I quickly dropped a tip into his jar, collected my drinks, and scooted out of there before he could impart any more wisdom on me. I'd had my fill of bartender parenting wisdom for one millennium.

As I made my way back toward where I'd left Rowen, I noticed she wasn't there. Assuming my mom or one of my sisters had snatched her the moment I'd left her side, I scanned the general vicinity where I'd last seen my parents and my younger sisters hanging out with a group of girls who were not-so-casually hanging around a group of boys. I'd seen Clementine and Hyacinth, but Lily was still MIA tonight. My mom hadn't told me directly where she was or who she was coming with—probably because she gave me a hard time for making angry faces when I had a smile like mine—but that didn't mean I hadn't figured it out. Lily was coming with Colt. She wasn't here yet with Colt. So where the hell were they? And what the hell were they doing? And why the hell did I feel like I wanted to hit something really hard?

I broke to a stop and closed my eyes, concentrating on calming down and caging the anger monkeys that had gotten loose. I hardly had enough energy to spend on Rowen and myself—what was I doing wasting any of it contemplating ways to dent Colt Mason's face?

The whole stop, close, and breathe thing seemed to work. At least until I spotted my wife with another guy. On the dance floor.

Where some guys might have preferred to find their wives dancing to a fast, sharp-beated song with a good amount of distance between her and the guy she was shaking with versus a slow one where space was in short, if any, supply, I felt the opposite. I moved through the crowd with new purpose, and my boots thundered across the dance floor a few moments later.

Neither of them saw me coming. They were both too busy having a good time and hooting, like the rest of the dancers, to notice me. I saw sweat starting to trickle down Rowen's neck and creep down her back.

"Whose brilliant idea was this?" I said when I jerked to a stop beside them.

Rowen's body slowed down enough to tell me my frustration wasn't going unnoticed. Her partner kept moving as he had been since I'd first seen them. They both pointed at the other in answer. I cocked a brow and waited. Their fingers stayed in the air, indicating at the other.

Finally, I knocked Garth's hat off of his head. "Come on, Black. What were you thinking?"

Garth shot a growl at me as he dived to retrieve his hat. "I was thinking your wife looked lonely and had been staring at this dance floor all night like she couldn't wait to bust a move." Garth motioned at Rowen after dropping his hat back on his head. "So . . . she's busting."

Actually, she'd stopped dancing almost completely. I knew she liked to dance, and I also knew she'd stopped doing something she liked because she knew I didn't like it, at least not in her present condition. Another shower of guilt dripped down on me when I realized I'd managed to inadvertently make Rowen's life smaller in my quest to preserve it. But what was I supposed to do? Stand by and say nothing while my pregnant wife with a life-threatening heart condition danced her tail off and dripped sweat in temperatures that had to be close to one hundred degrees at the center of the dance floor? I couldn't. I didn't know how.

Garth grabbed Rowen's hand and gave her a little spin. She started laughing.

"She's having a good time, Jess. Let it go. Rowen's tougher than you and me combined, and you know it." When Garth gave her another spin, he applied a bit too much force, and she wound up tripping on her own feet.

My arms were just snapping out to catch her or save her or do whatever they needed to do to help, but Garth readjusted her spin enough I wasn't needed. He'd saved her, and yes, if he hadn't, I would have been there as a second line of defense, but the incident had been enough to send another surge of frustration into my veins.

"You know she's pregnant, right?" When it looked like he was winding her up for another spin, I clapped my hand over his arm and lowered it.

"Oh, you mean that's why my best friend's turned into a nerve-racked homicidal maniac?" Garth continued to dance with Rowen, just in a more worried-husband-approved kind of way.

"Haven't realized the homicidal part yet, but I'm about to get there if you spin my pregnant wife one more time."

Garth took a good look at me, his shoulders slumping. "Look, I'm sorry, Jess. Really. I know Rowen's pregnant, and I know you're trying to treat her like she's some porcelain doll, but she looked like she needed to dance. And this is my party goddammit, and I wanted to dance too. So why don't you upend that beer so you can get shit-faced and totally forget the whole thing?"

At the reminder of the beer, I was reminded of the water. Shoving the extra one in my back pocket, I unscrewed the other one and handed it to Rowen. "Drink please."

She gave me a look but took the water. "Ditto." Her eyes dropped to my beer. "Please."

Garth watched me with that observant expression I wasn't used to seeing on him until lately. Whenever he looked at me like that, I felt as if he was inspecting a bomb about to explode and trying to decide which wire to cut to keep it from detonating.

"Where's Josie?" I asked, hoping if I found her, I could distract Garth from continuing to dance with Rowen.

"Close by," he answered.

"Don't you think you should find her? It is you guys's engagement party, right? Aren't you supposed to be together, you know, as an expression of your commitment to each other?"

Yeah, I was totally making that up as I went.

One side of Garth's face creased. "Unlike some guys I know, I don't feel the need to stifle the woman I love with my unending presence. We're okay being away from each other. You might want to work on that, Jess. Before Rowen gets sick of always being in your shadow."

When the skin between my brows creased, Rowen noticed it. She smiled and shook her head. "Getting sick of you? Not possible."

The blaring sound of the band came to a next-to-screeching halt, then broke into something slower and softer. Now that, that was better. Rowen's face ironed out with hope, giving me a look that required no words. I returned a look that needed no words either.

"I saved this one for you, Jess." Garth held out Rowen's hand for me, and I took it like I hadn't held it in months. Her hand was hot and damp too.

An MIA fiancée appeared over Garth's shoulder. "Dance with me, Black." Josie slung an arm around his neck and kissed the side of it, already swaying to the music despite the unconventional stance.

"With the way you just asked me, hell, I couldn't say no if you'd just handed me a knife and asked me to stab my heart with it." Garth tilted his head back so their faces were aligned before kissing her.

After a few moments of that, Rowen steered us away from them some. "I can't be that close to them when they're that *close* to each other."

A smile started to come over my face. The music had slowed, so had Rowen, and on the edge of the dance floor, it was cooler than an inferno. "A little PDA isn't so bad."

She blinked. "*That's* a little PDA?" As quickly as she'd glanced at Garth and Josie, she glanced away. "Yeah, and I'm a little pregnant."

By that point, Josie's hand was sneaking under Garth's shirt past his collar as their kissing entered the for-adults-only zone.

"They love each other. A lot. That's how they express it. It's not like they give a crap what anyone else thinks about how they show it." I pulled Rowen to me and wrapped her in my arms. Her hands found their spot behind my neck as her head settled against my chest. I felt like I was able to exhale some of the air I'd been holding for hours.

"I love you. A lot," she said, her words vibrating against my sternum. "I know I give those two a hard time about the public display thing, but if you ever wanted to, you know, give it a go . . ."

"What do you mean? I thought we already did."

Her head tipped up enough she could look at me. "Well, yeah, we kiss, we hug, we hold hands—"

"We slow dance," I added, moving her as slowly as I could and still be considered dancing instead of standing in place.

Her gaze roamed the masses around us. "What if we got crazy and added a little crazed kissing to our slow dancing and really spiced up our PDA repertoire?"

"That sounds a little . . . *crazed* . . . given your condition."

"Which condition are you referring to? The one

where I'm so sexually frustrated that when I finally implode, I'm going to become one gaping black hole in the galaxy?"

I looked around to see just how many people were getting an education in my wife's sexual frustration. Didn't look like anyone other than myself though.

"Because for *that* condition, crazed sounds ideal," she added.

When I started to think about what I could tell she was thinking about, it didn't take long before I'd arrived at the conclusion that crazed didn't only sound ideal, it sounded pretty damn tempting.

"It has been so long since I've seen that look on your face, I'd started to wonder if it was gone for good, but look at that"—Rowen's finger circled my face—"there it is in all its glory. The one that says one thousand different words, all of them deliciously filthy."

I didn't have a chance to respond before she grabbed my hand and started to pull me through the crowd toward the doors we'd come through. We were just about to them when a couple drifted in, finally making their appearance.

I broke to a stop, unsure what to do next. Then I noticed Lily's hair was more rumpled on one side, her cheeks were still flushed, and I knew exactly what to do.

CHAPTER five

Rowen

I WAS REALLY not going to catch a break during this pregnancy. The thought of Colt Mason being with his oldest sister about made steam plume from Jesse's ears, so getting to see them in real life—holding hands and wearing expressions just guilty enough to give away that they'd been making out—made him look like he was about to go nuclear.

When he'd broken to a stop after following me so willingly to whatever quiet, somewhat comfortable place I could find for us before I went nuclear due to lack of sexual anything, I'd tried tugging him forward. Then I tried pulling his wrist as I really dug my feet into the ground. I might as well have been trying to move the Great Wall of China. Jesse wasn't going anywhere.

"Maybe we should go say hi?" I suggested after giving the move-the-fortress thing one more try.

Jesse's reply was his expression darkening two more shades.

"Okay, maybe the mature one should go say hi," I mumbled as I started in Colt and Lily's direction.

"Rowen . . ." he called, not quite an order but several

degrees much too authoritative for my "I am woman, hear me roar and hyphenate my last name" liking.

"Jesse," I replied, hoping he heard the annoyed tone and caught it in my expression when I glanced back at him.

I wasn't just annoyed that my schemes for taking advantage of my husband had been foiled; I was also annoyed by his immature approach to Lily dating Colt. Jesse was typically chill and took a "live and let live" approach to those around him. It seemed, however, that whole "do what's right for you" methodology had a caveat—his sister dating a Mason.

I might not have punched my own personal stamp of ideal on Colt and Lily, but it didn't matter what I thought about the idealism of their relationship. At the moment, for the last few months of moments, both of them had obviously been in agreement that their relationship was more than ideal, and that was what mattered. I wanted Jesse to back down and remember what would have happened to us if we had listened to people's opinions on the idealism of our relationship at first. We never would have made it past day one, let alone gotten married.

I kept moving toward Colt and Lily. When they'd noticed me coming their way, they both smiled and started to close the gap between us, though I couldn't help noticing that every few steps, one of them would throw a hesitant glance over my shoulder at where I guessed Jesse was still fuming-meets-sulking.

Most of the time, I reminded myself why Jesse got so worked up about Lily's beau: he loved Lily and wanted the best for her. In his opinion, Colt Mason wasn't the best for her. In my opinion, I doubted that any man would be what

Jesse considered best for his sister. The same would hold true when Hyacinth and Clementine got to this stage. Actually, it would probably be worse since Lily was the calm, rational Walker sister, though if I were to ask Jesse, I knew he'd say she wasn't being rational in her choice of boyfriends.

I might not have been an objective party, but I felt I could at least be fair. Yes, Colt was older than Lily and maybe a bit too "California" for my country through-and-through husband's likes, but he was a good person, took such good care of her, and looked at her like idolizing her was his religion. That he'd stuck with her even after Jesse had made his disapproval of their relationship so well known I half-expected an article to be printed in the local paper about it said a lot about the feelings Colt had developed for her in a short amount of time.

Oh yeah, and there was the whole thing about Lily liking Colt and Colt liking Lily. They'd chosen each other, and for me, that was enough. It wasn't enough for my brooding husband though.

The closer I got to Colt and Lily, the more I felt Jesse's irritation rolling off of him. It didn't stop me though. If he wanted to continue making his stance on his sister's boyfriend evident, that was his prerogative. My prerogative was a tad different.

"Hey, you guys," I greeted when we were within a few feet of each other. "Nice of you two to finally show up all shifty-eyed with mussed tresses." I ran my fingers through the side of Lily's hair. It was such blaring piece of evidence of what they'd been doing, I came close to blushing as I untangled the knots. "Mirror. Brush." I finished smoothing the last tangles. "Check it and use it next time."

Colt shifted beside Lily while she averted her eyes from my pointed stare.

"How have you guys been?" I asked as I gave Lily a hug. She gave firmer hugs now. I didn't know why I noticed, because it seemed like a small thing, but ever since she started dating Colt, she embraced people with a bit more purpose. "Besides all tangled up around each other in Colt's truck?"

When I bounced my eyebrows, Colt shifted again. Lily didn't shift though; she rolled her eyes. Go figure the guy who'd convinced an entire town he'd made ego his bitch was the one shifting in place, while the girl who'd made an art out of blending in with the walls was the one rolling her eyes.

"We're great," Lily answered, her eyes lowering to my stomach once they were done revolving. "How are *you* doing?"

"I'm doing good." As a policy, I rarely, if ever, gave vanilla answers to any kind of question, but I was fresh out of colorful responses to that question. But *How are you?* weighted with just enough enunciation to imply disaster was tiptoeing behind me? I got asked that question a lot.

"How did your appointment go?" Lily asked.

"It went good." Another vanilla response. I was just so tired of talking about me and the unsaid of what might happen sitting beneath the surface of every similar question. I knew people asked because they cared and were concerned—I knew I'd be doing the same if situations were reversed—but I'd answered enough questions about how I was doing and how my appointments had gone to last my next ten lifetimes. I needed a break. I needed to talk about someone else's issues instead of my own.

My gaze lingered on where Colt and Lily's hands were joined. Colt was a big guy, and Lily was small for a woman. I would have expected Colt's hand to swallow Lily's entirely, but instead—with their fingers laced together as they were—they looked close to the same size. "We've got to figure out what to do about your brother."

"I agree. He hasn't been looking good, or even healthy, for months." Lily's gaze drifted behind me to where I guessed Jesse was still stewing in his boots. "He's worried about you though. I don't think he'll get past this until you've delivered and both you and the baby are okay."

I smiled at Lily. She might have changed in some ways, in some *good* ways, but she was still about as sweet and selfless as they came. Where she'd thought I'd been referring to Jesse needing help pertaining to me, I'd actually meant he needed help regarding her and her choice of boyfriends.

"Don't worry—I've got that covered. I'm going to start slipping Xanax into his coffee in the morning and another in his cup with dinner. He'll be a happy, unconcerned potato for the next few months." I angled myself beside Lily just enough so I could see Jesse. He was in the same spot, arms crossed and body rigid. His expression was the same—cross and rigid. "But that's not anxiety right there. That's unbridled fury. Boundless anger bordering on rage. There isn't a pill for that."

As quickly as Lily looked at her brother, she looked away. I knew it was difficult for her to know that her big brother didn't approve of her boyfriend. I knew she felt as though she'd disappointed him in some way and that it killed her. I also knew she wouldn't give up someone she cared about because someone else she cared about wanted her to. It was in notions like that one that I saw more of myself in Lily than not.

"I don't know what to do. I've tried talking to him." Lily absently played with the hem of her dress as she stole another glance at her brother. "But all he ever answers with is him not wanting to talk about Colt and me in the same sentence, or he gets up and leaves the room." She exhaled what sounded like weeks of emotional weight. "I can't talk to him because talking requires the other party to actually engage in conversation."

"Okay, so the talking plan's a bust. Why don't you try something else?"

Colt and Lily looked at me, waiting.

"Why don't you try *showing* him instead?"

"Showing him what?" Colt asked, shuffling in closer so the three of us formed a loose circle.

"What your relationship is about." I lifted a shoulder. "He's under the impression you're no good for one another and that your relationship could never work. You guys are under a different impression, so why don't you show him that?"

Lily's brows pinched together. "How do we show him that when he's having a tough time being in the same ginormous barn packed with people as Colt? Not sure that'll work if we show up at breakfast tomorrow and try to slide into the chairs across from him."

From prior experience, I knew that was true. Jesse had never said anything disrespectful to their faces, but his actions couldn't be considered respectful. The last time we'd been in town and Colt and Lily had showed up to the Walker kitchen table at dinnertime, Jesse had dropped his napkin into his chair and claimed he had to finish watering the livestock. The time before that, a few fence posts had needed fixing. The time before that, the barn needed a fresh coat of paint. When it came to suffering though a meal with Colt, Jesse had no shortage of excuses for slipping out at the last minute.

"So how about when I see you guys making your way to the table tomorrow morning, I'll plop down in Jesse's lap, and we'll see if he's able to escape so swiftly then?"

Lily giggled at the picture playing out in her mind. "I like your creativity, but I'm not sure it would work."

"Why? I think it sounds like an outstanding plan." When I glanced at Colt to see if I could get him to join my side, I found all his attention was focused on Jesse. Yeah, because making eye contact and challenging the fuming man balancing precariously on the ledge of sanity was a bright idea.

"Well, because Jesse has been throwing around bales of hay and bags of feed like he was juggling snap peas since middle school. I doubt maneuvering the tiniest pregnant woman I've ever seen off his lap is going to slow him down from making his escape." Lily motioned at my stomach like she was proving her point.

I looked down to see if I'd gone from size Saturn to size Pluto. Nope. My stomach was still creating its own gravitational field. "It's worth a try, oh you of little faith." I thrust my hand behind my back. "And it's better than letting these two continue their stare off from fifty feet apart."

Lily chewed it out on her lower lip, her gaze shifting between her brother and her boyfriend as if she was contemplating how to go about mixing oil with vinegar.

"Okay, so if this is going to work, it's going to take more than just you dropping into Jesse's lap to get him to stay in his chair at breakfast tomorrow." She continued to nibble on her lip as her eyes narrowed in concentration. "You better squirt a few rings of super glue onto his chair too. Just to be safe."

I bumped my arm against hers and smiled. "Already so two steps ahead of you. I've shuffled through the gray matter where useless information is kept and dusted off the file listing where your dad keeps his tubes of glue"—I tapped my temple—"as well as a hammer and nails to secure the legs of his chair to the kitchen floor so he won't think about escaping with the chair glued to his ass."

That made Lily laugh again. "You're right. You are two steps ahead of me."

When I joined in with her laughter, only laughing harder as we glanced between the two stone-cold expressions on Jesse and Colt's faces, I felt it again. Harder. Stronger. That stomach-tightening-before-snapping sensation hit me so hard it sent me back a couple of steps.

"Hey? Rowen?" Lily's laughter cut off instantly as she reached for my arm. "What's the matter?"

Colt had come around to my other side, one arm going around my back to support me as he exchanged a nervous look with Lily.

That one had been painful enough it probably would have dropped me to my knees if Lily and Colt hadn't been on me like white on rice. As sudden and staggering as it had been, it passed as quickly as it had come on. Barely a handful of seconds had passed, and the rip-me-open sensation was gone.

And so was the guy guarding his post fifty feet away.

"What happened?" Jesse asked in a tone hinging on scared shitless when he broke to a stop in front of us.

Lily shook her head, studying me with her own mask of worry. I knew she and Jesse weren't related by blood, but that didn't change the fact that almost two decades of growing up together meant they could practically mirror each other's facial expressions. Her worry lines folded as deep and in as many places as Jesse's.

"I don't know. She didn't say," Lily said.

"Rowen, what's going on?" Jesse stayed right in front of me, not seeming to notice Colt camped out beside me, still ready to support me if my body gave out again.

I paused before answering because this one required some deliberation. Whatever that hell-fire sensation had been, it had gotten my attention. It had even made me a bit nervous. I'd been feeling clusters of something similar all night, but in comparison, those had been weak tremors. This had been like the ten on the Richter scale.

I sucked in a breath and did a quick check of how I felt now. Fine. Normal. Whatever that had been was gone and didn't seem to be coming back. It might not have been wise or smart or cautious, but looking into my husband's anxious face, which looked one answer away from breaking, I forced a smile.

"Indigestion," I said in that calm, even voice I'd perfected ten lifetimes ago. Faking one emotion for another . . . Spiderman could scale sky-scrapers, I had that. "That's what's going on."

Jesse shook his head hard. "You're lying."

Lily sucked in a tiny breath beside me.

I weaved out of Lily and Colt's holds and stepped toward Jesse. "You just called me a liar."

"I said you were lying, not that you are a liar."

"That's the same thing."

"No, it's not." Jesse rubbed at his temples. "That's like saying you took a paperclip from the bank, so you're a klepto."

Fine, he had a point, but I wished he didn't. I couldn't keep arguing circles around him and distracting him from what was important if he proved his point in one succinct statement.

"Are you going to tell me what happened just now? Or do I have to haul you to the emergency room and have the doctor on call there tell me what happened?" Jesse stopped rubbing his temples long enough to give me one of his sweeping inspections. His gaze lingered on my stomach.

I didn't want to go to the E.R. I wanted to stay right there and enjoy the night and our friends and family and each other. I didn't want to ruin Garth and Josie's special night because my body had done something a little crazy and my husband had taken that whole crazy thing and run with it. I didn't want to be treated as if I was hanging from a thread and everyone was holding their breaths, waiting for it to snap. I didn't want my husband to hold me at arm's length in some areas while he held me so close I felt like I was suffocating in others.

I didn't want to leave.

"I already told you. Indigestion. Too many taquitos. Too few Tums." I paused to take a breath because damn if it wasn't exhausting being pregnant in a hot barn smashed to capacity with people while I tried to convince my husband for the one millionth time that I wasn't seconds away from taking my last breath. "I'm fine."

Jesse was looking at me like I was anything but fine. Colt was too. Lily though? There was warmth in her eyes and a smile on her face. She was on my side. Two against two. That might have been even in a different situation, but this was two men versus two *women*. The very same women they loved, cared for, and got their making out dot, dot, dot needs satisfied from—or at least *had* until Jesse had gone all old-school monk on me—so we weren't tied. No, Lily and my vote won. The guys knew it too.

"I think I need another bottle of water," I said to Jesse.

He gave me an exasperated expression that said he knew exactly what I meant—he needed another bottle of beer.

"Walker," Colt cut in, like Jesse and I weren't in the middle of a hydration stand-off.

Jesse's eyes cut to Colt—long enough to express some serious displeasure—before landing back on me. "Mason."

I lifted my eyes to the barn ceiling. I didn't know why they even acknowledged each other if that was how they did it every time they ran into one another. Puffing out my chest and narrowing my eyes at Lily, I channeled whatever gruffness I had. "Walker."

She giggled but managed to stifle it quickly. Lifting her head, Lily rolled her shoulders back and settled her hands on her hips as Colt had them. "Sterling-Walker."

My eyes widened before I nodded at Lily's seriously impressive talent at playing the part of a twenty-something guy. "That was impressive, Lily. You win that round."

"Really?" she said, going back to herself seamlessly. "I thought it was a tad overacted. You know, the sneer thing might have been a bit much."

I made it a point to inspect both Colt and Jesse's faces. "Eh, no. You nailed it."

Lily and I were in the middle of high-fiving when Jesse and Colt shook their heads.

"We don't sound, look, or act anything like that," Colt piped up first, flinging his finger between Lily and me.

"Yeah, you pretty much do." Lily patted Colt's arm in an attempt to console him, but when his frown only grew, she just shrugged.

"Nothing like that," Jesse added, though his eyes were still zeroed in on my stomach.

"*Everything* like that," I argued.

Jesse sighed, but he was clearly already over the disagreement and ready to get back to why I'd nearly done a back-flop into Colt's arms.

"What's going on?" he asked again, lowering his voice.

"Nothing."

He shook his head and set his jaw. I shouldn't have looked away when I answered him. That was standard procedure for what a person shouldn't do when attempting to lie.

"Rowen . . ."

That tone made me bristle a bit more each time he used it.

"Come on, Jesse, ease off," Lily said. "She's okay now. Why don't you enjoy the party?"

"I was enjoying the party until you two showed up and my wife looked like she was about to pass out."

My eyes went wide at his words. Jesse had always

been gentle to a fault with his sisters, Lily especially. I knew his words came from a place of worry and were directed at Colt's presence, not hers, but still . . . the hurt on her face went deep. She wasn't used to masking her emotions like some of us were.

"Hey, Walker. Back off." Colt stepped forward, putting Lily just enough behind him to look like he was ready to protect her from a firing squad.

Jesse didn't miss it either. "My sister doesn't need you to take care of her, Mason. She's perfectly capable of taking care of herself."

"I never said she wasn't." Colt's hands fell from his hips down to his sides, his fingers curling into his palms. Jesse's had been curled in the same way since Colt had shown up. "Rowen's pretty damn capable of taking care of herself too, you know. She doesn't need you calling the cavalry and playing hero every time she trips on something."

Jesse's jaw ground together. Then he stepped toward Colt. If either of them took another step, they'd be bumping chests. Jesse and Colt were built the same: tall, wide shoulders, muscular, although Jesse's were the kind developed from hard work and labor whereas Colt's had been hewn in a weight room. I didn't want to see either of them get in a fight with anyone, least of all each other. While I knew neither was predisposed to testosterone-fueled fights, nothing about that day had gone with the flow.

"Back off, Walker," Colt said, though his feet stayed in place.

"Lily's my sister. I'm her brother. I'm not backing off. You are."

Lily and I exchanged another look. Where was Garth

Black when I needed him? He could ease the tension by yapping some lewd comment before sending them on their separate ways or if they did get into it, act as a scrappy enough referee to tear them apart.

"I'm her boyfriend." Colt's chest went out a bit—the whole scene reminded me that Freud was right on so many levels. "I'm not going anywhere."

"You and Lily have been dating for all of five minutes. Don't make grand proclamations you can't be certain you're capable of keeping."

I wasn't used to seeing Jesse so confrontational. I wasn't sure I liked it. Was this side of him brought on from the stress of the pregnancy? Or would this be the norm for him no matter which of his sisters' boyfriends was standing in front of him? I didn't know. All I did know was that I needed to drag Jesse away from Colt, or Lily had to drag Colt away from Jesse. Those two wouldn't be friends anytime this decade.

"We've been dating almost six months, and I have every confidence I can back what I just said." Colt reached for Lily's hand, not blinking as he stared down Jesse. "I'm not going anywhere."

Before Jesse could snap back with anything else, I grabbed his hand and pulled him away. "We're going somewhere though. Somewhere else." I waved at Lily as I continued to wrestle the wall of determination away from the future scene of the crime. "*Anywhere* else," I added when I noticed how tight Jesse's fists were curled.

Thankfully, he didn't resist much or I wouldn't have been able to tug him into the far side of the barn.

"You don't want to alienate your sister, right?" I asked when we stopped. I felt the stirrings of a side-ache from the effort it had taken to haul Jesse halfway across the barn.

Jesse's gaze flickered to where Colt and Lily were starting to mingle into the crowd. It took a minute, but he finally shook his head. "No. I don't."

"Then you need to change the way you behave around her when Colt's around because you going all crazed ape, pounding your chest and grunting, is going to alienate her a bit more every time." I rubbed at my side to ease the tension pulling my muscles tight. I hadn't experienced a side-ache like this since I'd had to take the dreaded mile test in gym class.

When he watched Lily with Colt again, he seemed to appraise them with a different set of eyes, ones that weren't prejudiced but investigative. His face flattened as he studied his sister and her boyfriend like they were any other couple in the room. Of course that was when Colt dropped his hands to Lily's hips, drew her close, and lowered his mouth to hers. His mouth stayed there for a while too.

After about five seconds, Jesse took a step in their direction again. "He's crossed the line now. I'm going to remind him where that line is."

Before he could take another step, I snagged the back of his shirt and kept him in place. "Kissing your girlfriend of six months is crossing the line? Really?" I gave his shirt another tug when Jesse lunged forward when Colt's hand wove into Lily's hair and pressed her closer to him. "Because if that's the case, what do you consider what we did in that attic bedroom of yours before we were even 'official'? Pole-vaulting over the line? Being fired out of a cannon over the line? Lighting a stick of dynamite and obliterating the line?"

Jesse's shoulders lowered before he glanced back at me. "I knew I loved you. You knew the same. We didn't need to ascribe a title to it to know that. I made love with you that night because I *loved* you."

My stomach fluttered a little. Brooding and anxious and everything in between, and he could still manage to say just the right thing. "And you don't think Colt and Lily love each other?"

Jesse snorted as if the concept were preposterous. With the way they looked at each other, paired with the way they didn't seem to notice anyone else when they were together, it didn't seem so outlandish to me.

He thrust his hand in their direction, where they were still kissing. "She's seventeen. He's, like, thirty. That's a recipe for a felony, not true love."

His back was still to me, so I rolled my eyes. "Lily is seventeen for one more month. Colt's your age, and if you're thirty, then damn, I married a sugar daddy."

I could just make out a smirk forming on Jesse's face. "Well, for one more month, it's illegal."

"It's not illegal to love someone. No matter the age difference."

Jesse's back went rigid. "He doesn't love her."

"Alienation. Just say no." Lily loved her brother, but I knew how teenage girls worked. If Jesse made her choose between him and Colt, Jesse would be in for the shock of his life.

His flames were starting to stifle. He didn't look like every muscle in his body was one flex away from bursting through his skin.

Of course that was when Garth jogged up to us with a

pissed off expression, his thumb pointing over his shoulder. "Would you rather me kick his ass or throw his ass out, Jess? Your call."

"Hi, Garth. Great to see you. Impeccable timing." I folded my arms. "I'd just managed to talk Hulk out of his green skin, and now he's quivering and mottling green again."

"Seeing him with Lily makes my skin crawl. Maybe if his face isn't so pretty, the spell she's under will be broken. My vote's for the ass beating." Garth shouldered up beside Jesse as if the two were deliberating how best to get a herd of cattle to forge a river.

"Lily isn't some shallow girl who goes all wobbly-kneed over a pretty face. She's not into him because he's hot."

Two heads twisted back to look at me.

"Are you saying you think Colt Mason's 'hot'?" Garth asked, already inspecting me like I was a traitor.

"No. I'm paraphrasing what you said. You're the one who called him hot." My side hurt again, but I couldn't grab at it with Jesse looking at me.

"I did not call him hot."

"It's okay. You can think he's hot. I won't judge." I raised a shoulder and focused on keeping a straight face. It was a rare day when I could get a reaction out of Garth Black, and I wasn't in a hurry for it to pass.

Garth turned around to face me straight-on. "If I was into dudes, I know for a fact pretty-boy, pansy-ass Colt Mason wouldn't be my type."

"What would be Garth Black's type because this, I've got to hear." I leaned into the wall and waited.

Garth shifted before whacking the back of his hand

into Jesse's chest. "This guy. A true blue cowboy who doesn't know about things like facials and Paleo and all things of a metro nature."

"What's Paleo?" I dusted off the spot on Jesse's chest that Garth had thumped. "And please refrain from touching my husband in any sort of way—whacks, smacks, slugs, and handshakes included—after spilling about you jumping his bones if you pitched for the other team."

Instead of squirming in his boots as I hoped he would, Garth slid a little closer to Jesse and batted his eyes at him. "Why? You jealous, Sterling-Walker? Can't take a little healthy competition?"

"Whatever that is"—I motioned at Garth about to drool while still batting his eyes at Jesse, who was not-so-subtly edging away—"unlike Paleo, there is nothing healthy about it."

"I thought you didn't know what Paleo was." Garth fired off one especially salacious wink at Jesse before going out of hots-for-Jesse character and back into hots-for-Josie character.

"I live in Seattle, where so many carrots and sweet potatoes are consumed, people walk down crowded, dreary streets looking like orange-faced oompa loompas. Of course I know what Paleo is." Not that I followed it, because this girl might be able to give up most kinds of meat, but do not ask me to drop sugar. Wasn't happening. "What I want to know is how you know what Paleo is."

Garth shifted in place. Of course talking about some diet would make him uncomfortable when acting like he was nursing a semi for his best friend wouldn't. "I don't know. I probably read about it in some magazine in some doctor's office. I spent enough time waiting in those aptly named 'waiting' rooms to become an expert in which haircuts are best for a person's face shape, how to pick the right red lipstick for your skin tone, and what little black dress is best for your body type . . . and other useless shit like that."

I leaned in, scrutinizing his lips or, more accurately, what was sparkling on his lips. "I don't know about the red lipstick thing, but you really nailed the right shade of pink lip gloss. Nailed. It."

The back of Garth's hand was wiping and patting his lips so quickly, I'd have thought I'd just told him they were on fire. "That's Josie's lip shit. Not mine."

"*Sure,* it isn't, Brokeback. Sure, it isn't."

Jesse exhaled and shook his head—standard procedure for when Garth and I got into it like this.

Garth slid in my direction, pinning me to the wall with his unblinking stare. "You can call me Brokeback all you want. I'll smile and take it while calling you little Ms. Pregnant-and-Barefoot Suzi Homemaker."

"Ouch," I said, reaching for the place where the sharp pain in my side was stabbing me.

"'Ouch' is right. You're not the only one who can break out the name calling, Sterling-Walker." Garth was grinning in victory, not getting it, but the lightness fading from Jesse's face gave away that he had.

Another stab hit me, doubling me over. "Ouch." This time I sounded more like I'd just taken a wrecking ball to the gut. I would have fallen to my knees if Jesse hadn't swooped in and saved me, only further securing his spot in the Hero Hall of Fame.

Only when Jesse had to save me from face-planting did Garth get it. "Holy shit, I'm an asshole." He rushed toward us, his arms moving like he wanted to help but wasn't sure how. "What can I do?"

"Go get my truck!" Jesse hollered, gathering me into his arms while I attempted to grit my teeth and not cry out when another stab attacked me.

"Shouldn't we call 9-1-1 or something?" Garth sounded about as flustered as I'd ever heard him as he started to clear a path through the crowd. Thankfully we were close to one of the exits, so it wouldn't take long to get outside.

"No paramedic can get here then to the emergency room quicker than I can. I know every way to get to the hospital from here, and the quickest way based on the time of day. Or night," Jesse added as he rushed through the barn.

"That relict of a truck of yours belongs in a museum, Jess, not speeding down a maze of dirt roads toward a hospital thirty minutes away when your wife looks like she's dying." Garth grimaced when Jesse and I threw him looks ranging from irritated to irate. "Figuratively speaking, of course." He shoved a couple of guys out of the way, shaking his head. "I'm not only an asshole—I'm an insensitive one too."

"You can't have one without the other." I had to concentrate on taking a breath before I could add anything else. "Don't feel too bad."

As Jesse carried me through the big barn doors, he glanced at Garth, who was keeping pace with us. "Can you tell my parents what happened and where we're going? They'll worry when they realize we're gone."

Garth nodded as he pulled keys from his pocket. "I'll call and let them know once we're at the hospital."

"What are you talking about?" Jesse's pace picked up when he took another look at my face . . . and I was trying to disguise how much pain I was in.

"I'm driving you guys. That's what I'm talking about." Garth's sleek black truck roared to a start when he punched a button on the key, and unlike Old Bessie, it was right in front of us.

"No. It's your engagement party. I can't let you leave it to chauffeur us to the hospital." Where Jesse's words said he wouldn't allow it, his body jogged toward Garth's truck.

"Yeah, and it's been fan-fucking-tastic, but one of my good friends looks like she's being drawn and quartered, and my other good friend, in case he's forgotten, has been drinking way too much for his pathetically low tolerance to get behind a wheel and drive." When we broke to a stop in front of Garth's truck, he threw open the passenger side door and waved Jesse toward it. When Jesse hesitated, Garth took a step toward us, looking like he was trying to work out how to throw us both in his truck if it came to it. "My truck's right here. It's newer, faster, safer, and only about a thousand times less likely to sputter out and die on the way there. I also happen to be a better driver." Garth spun his keys around his fingers. "I was a race car driver in another life."

Jesse took a tentative step toward the swung-open door, his gaze wandering from the barn, where the party was still vibrating from, to Garth's steely look of determination, to me, who was just focusing on not crying out each time my body was rocked by that vise-like sensation that was attempting to flatten my insides into crepe-sized pieces.

"Your party . . ." Jesse bowed his head but kept moving toward Garth's truck.

"This isn't about me or the party or any of that right now." Garth stepped aside when Jesse came around the passenger door. "This is about Rowen and your baby and getting them as safely and quickly to the hospital as we can."

Jesse nodded as he lifted me into the cushy backseat that was, thank God, a big bench seat. I dragged myself to the end of it and curled my legs to my stomach to make room for Jesse, who had already leapt in the back with me and was crawling across the truck floor toward my head.

"Hang in there. We're on our way. Garth will get us to the hospital in fifteen minutes flat with the way he drives." Jesse's anxious whispers kept beat to his hand running down the length of my hair.

He was trying to soothe me, to comfort me and tell me everything would be okay. I wanted to return the favor, but this was one of the few times I couldn't pretend things would be okay. Nothing felt okay with the way my body was raging some kind of internal war.

Garth leapt into the driver's seat and had just punched the gas when the truck rolled to a stop. I heard the whir of a window going down, filling the cab with cool, fresh air. That, combined with pressing my cheek into the cool leather seat, helped calm the inferno blazing through my body. I felt like something had found a dozen dusty old furnaces inside me and fired them up, notching the dial to its upper range.

"Thatta girl! Kick off those boots and run!" Garth shouted, revving the engine a couple of times.

From the end of his last rev to when I heard the passenger door groaning open before someone threw themselves inside, a mere half second had passed, if that.

"Colt and Lily told me they'd seen you three leaving the party like the devil was chasing you." Josie was breathing hard, practically panting. "I wasn't sure if it was because you'd changed your mind and were fleeing for Mexico, or if something else had happened . . ." After landing a soft smack into Garth's arm, Josie's head appeared above me. Her eyes went wide when she saw the scene in the backseat. "Fuck me," she said in a long exhale. She threw another slug into Garth's arm. "Drive. Fast."

Climbing over the back of her seat, Josie landed on top of Jesse with a thud, but that didn't slow her down. She managed to wedge herself into a small space beside my head. Worry lines stitched into Josie's face as she ran her hand down my forehead. "What's going on?"

The truck was hauling ass, and the one great thing about Garth's fancy new truck was that the ride was smooth in comparison to Old Bessie. The gentle vibration of potholes as we sped down Garth and Josie's driveway would have felt like being spin-cycled in Old Bessie.

"Come on, Rowen. Talk to me." Josie got in my face and stroked my forehead. Beside her, I saw Jesse's chest rising and falling hard.

"I feel like I've got a boa constrictor wrapping around me, doing its thing—that's what's the matter." Getting that out took far too much effort. I was feeling light-headed too . . . which meant I wasn't getting enough oxygen . . . which meant my heart was struggling . . . which meant . . .

"Faster, Garth. Please," I squeaked, but I wasn't sure if Josie heard, let alone Garth in the front seat barreling down the street.

Twisting around, Josie stuck her head next to Garth's. "Baby, you know I love you, but I swear to god, if you don't take the lead out and move this thing, I will have to insist on taking the wheel."

The engine fired louder as the truck picked up speed. Jesse had to grab onto the back of the front seat to brace himself, but he still managed to get a seat belt fastened around me with one hand.

"Hey, Mama Bear. You hang in there, okay?" Garth glanced back like he was afraid he would find blood and guts splattered around the backseat.

"Eyes on the road, babe. Not going to be helpful if we wind up in a ditch and all clog up the emergency room tonight." Josie spun his head back around before crouching beside me. She had to shoulder Jesse out of the way to fit.

"Hanging," I answered Garth.

Jesse threw off his hat and shoved his hair back. His hands slowly moved toward me—one covered my heart, the other formed around my stomach. "It's going to be okay. I'm here. You'll be fine. The baby will be fine." His voice was even, calm, spoken like he was reciting a mantra. His eyes gave him away though. They always did. "I won't let anything happen. Nothing."

Lifting my hand to his face felt like I was bench pressing an elephant, but I managed it. "I know, Jesse. I know." I held his gaze for a moment, trying to impress my feigned confidence on him, then I had to close them. I felt like the elephant was now pushing down on my eyelids.

A few silent minutes passed after that. That sharp, tightening sensation increased in frequency to the point it felt like I'd only just managed to catch my breath before another one pressed down upon me.

Jesse's hands stayed in their spots while Josie never stopped stroking my face. Her mouth lowered to just outside of my ear, and she whispered so softly, I barely made it out. "Is it the baby or your heart?"

I took a breath before answering, checking to make sure Jesse hadn't picked up on Josie's question. My response was just as quiet. "The baby."

She swallowed then stared out the window. Tension filled the cab of the truck to the point I felt like I was about to suffocate. That was when the truck took a sharp turn.

"E.R. ahead," Garth announced.

The breaths Josie and Jesse had been holding came out at the same time in a never-ending rush.

"Thank you, Garth," Jesse whispered, his voice on the cusp of trembling. "I owe you."

Garth rolled to a stop at what I guessed were the E.R. doors. "Yeah, yeah. I'll add it to your owe-me tab. Just get her in there and demand an army of the best doctors check her out before I park and make my way in there." Garth leapt out of the truck and opened the driver's side door. He helped Josie hop out first. "Because if I come in there and find her like this in that waiting room, I'm going to start busting heads, and I won't stop until someone lights a fire under their ass."

Jesse gave a quick nod as he unbuckled my seat belt and tried to move me. I tried to help by leaning up on my elbow, but the strength had left my body. Something had held a vacuum to just the right spot and sucked it all away. Where my strength had escaped, Jesse's had multiplied. He wrapped his arms around me and curled me to his chest like he was cradling nothing more substantial than a lamb before climbing out of the truck. Garth and Josie were stationed on either side of us, I guess ready to catch us if we fell, but I wasn't sure I'd ever felt Jesse so steady.

His boots had barely hit the pavement before he ran toward the E.R. doors. His hat was still missing, so his long tufts of hair bounced with every stride, falling into his eyes before lifting again. With the fluorescent lights shining above us and me looking up at him, Jesse looked more ethereal than human. Like he belonged to a different world, a better one.

"I need a doctor!" he shouted as he approached the admitting area. "My wife. She's pregnant. Her heart. She needs help." His voice wasn't trembling anymore—it echoed through the vast area, filling the empty space with his words.

My vision went blurry, a lot like it had that day I'd been running around the track and decided to see how fast I could get around it. Right before I passed out.

I heard what sounded like a bunch of shuffling as a stretcher seemed to magically appear beside me. Someone told Jesse to stay in the waiting room, but he had a few choice words for them. His hand slipped into mine, and it stayed there the whole time I was wheeled into a room. It stayed there when a herd of doctors and nurses descended on me, poking, prodding, and hooking me up to so many machines, I felt like more of a robot than a person by the end of it.

Jesse's hand had gotten me through so many tough times. It didn't falter as I went through what would prove to be my toughest either.

CHAPTER six

Jesse

THEY WANTED ME to leave. They'd told me to leave. They'd ordered me to leave.

I was still here.

I didn't know how these nurses and doctors could just expect people to leave the ones they love because they'd asked that person to. I didn't know why they'd even expect a husband to go quietly back to the waiting room while his wife and child were in trouble. Maybe it worked sometimes. It didn't work this time though.

Screw protocol, procedure, and policy. I wasn't leaving Rowen.

The swirl of doctors and nurses didn't seem to stop, all of them rushing in and out, rolling in new machines each time. By the end of the initial whirlwind, Rowen was attached to a heart rate monitor—actually two, one for her heart and one for the baby's—an oxygen mask, and an I.V. with a couple of different bags dripping into her veins. The baby's heartbeat was so fast—so strong—in comparison to hers. Rowen's sounded slow and weak, like it was dwindling down to its last beat. I didn't think I stopped staring at that heart rate monitor until the buzz of medical staff had calmed to a gentle trickle and a woman carried in a clipboard of paperwork.

"So you're the stubborn one." She was close to my mom's age and had perfected the fine workings of the "Mom look" as was evidenced by the one she aimed my way.

I answered with a non-committal shrug and took the clipboard when she handed it over.

"Well, I see why the nurses didn't insist security throw you into the waiting room where you belong." She lowered her reading glasses as she took a good look at me. She followed that up with a shake of her head.

"Why's that?"

She shook her head again. "For the same reason they're in the break room, fanning themselves and talking in high-pitched squeals."

I clicked the pen and filled in the first box. Name: Rowen Sterling-Walker. "Because they're hot?"

The lady gave a sudden laugh before walking away. "They're hot all right."

I didn't spend any more time trying to decipher what she was implying. I focused on filling in every column of every page of the dozen sheets attached to the clipboard. Most were front and back. Paperwork wasn't typically my thing, but I didn't mind it so much right now. It gave me a temporary distraction from the beeping machines and dripping I.V.s, and it made me feel as though I was useful for one thing at least, instead of feeling utterly useless as I would if I were just sitting there, holding her hand, and holding my breath while hoping that everything would be okay. I was on the back of the last page when one of the doctors from earlier slipped back into the room.

"We're going to move her upstairs," he announced, inspecting the machines and Rowen and just about everything else as he spoke to me. "We'll keep her for a couple of days to make sure she and the baby stay stable, then we'll send her home." His inspection of his patient complete, his gaze shifted my way. "Are you the father?"

My brows pinched together. Raising my left hand, I pointed at the gold band circling my finger. "I'm her husband."

The doctor didn't even blink. "Are you the *baby's* father?"

That was why he was looking at me like I was an asshole. "Oh, yeah." I nodded, staring at Rowen's stomach. "I am."

"Great. And since I already know you're her husband, I can skip the next question on my list." The doctor spoke in one of the most monotone voices I'd ever heard. I didn't think people generally used that word to describe a person's expression, but if a person could have a monotone expression, the doctor had nailed the mastery of it.

"I'm *her* husband and *the baby's* father." I felt like I was stating the obvious, like telling him E.R. rooms weren't a peaceful, happy place.

"Thanks for clearing that up. Sorry I had to ask, but you'd be surprised how many husbands we get in here who aren't the ones who fathered the children inside their wife's uterus."

I shifted in my chair. Something about hearing the word uterus in the same statement circling around adultery was all kinds of awkward.

"What happened?" I clicked the pen a few times, as

afraid of the question as I was of the answer. "Exactly?"

Everyone had been so busy since we'd showed up, myself included, that I still didn't know exactly what had happened to put us here. Other than Rowen looking like her insides were being ripped apart, piece by piece, while she struggled to take a solid breath, I didn't know what had happened. I guessed it had something to do with her heart, but I wasn't sure exactly.

The doctor gave me a strange look, like he was surprised by my question or that I had to ask it. "Your wife went into early labor."

I leaned back in the chair. "She's not due for three months though."

"That's why we were all rushing around like a child's life depended on it." The doctor motioned around the room, continuing on in that monotone voice that seemed close to tipping the tired scale. "Because it was."

"But the baby . . ." I automatically checked the fetal heart rate monitor. "It's okay now, right?"

"Yes, it's fine, and even if we hadn't been able to stop the labor and your baby had been delivered today, chances are good it would have been okay too. It would have been in the NICU for a few weeks, of course, but statistically speaking, your baby had a very good chance of surviving a preterm labor." He lifted a brow, almost like he was challenging me to ask another question.

I bit my tongue. Instead of firing off a half dozen qualifying questions, peppering in a few less-than-kind words, I inhaled a deep breath. I told myself these E.R. doctors and nurses probably saw dozens of patients on every shift. Some of them made it, some didn't. They had to find a way to distance themselves from the patients and their families to keep from going crazy. I got that. I could sympathize even.

But this was *my* wife. *My* child. They weren't just one of the dozens for the night or hundreds for the month. They were my whole entire world.

"Will we have a different doctor when we get moved upstairs?" I didn't blink as I addressed the doctor.

He nodded.

"Then when can we move?"

I didn't know if he took the hint or just needed to move on to a different patient, but he didn't say anything else before leaving the room. I exhaled after he was gone. I probably should have felt bad for being less than courteous with one of the people responsible for helping my wife and unborn child, but I couldn't seem to conjure up much sympathy for a person when it was clear his concern and compassion were in the lacking zone.

By the time I'd finished the last few columns on the back page, a couple of nurses popped back into the room.

"Damn. Thank God for drawing the long straws," the light-haired nurse said, nudging the dark-haired one beside her.

"I'm thanking God for a lot more than that if you know what I mean," the other replied.

"Like tight jeans and men who don't mind wearing them?"

"It's like you're reading my mind."

It was like they thought they were the only two people in the room and I wasn't standing a whole ten feet in front of them.

"Wasting your time, girls," another nurse scoffed as she shouldered through them. "This one likes a different kind of nurse." She didn't glance back, but she must have guessed their expressions had shifted into the confused spectrum. "The *male* kind." She fired a wink at me.

It had been years since I'd graduated from high school, but my class had had a whole thirty-two students. I could see any one of them fifty years from now in the most unlikely of places and probably still remember their name. Katy had grown up a few farms down from ours, and both of her big brothers had worked for my dad when they came home from college in the summers. We'd never been particularly good friends, but that was mainly because I was too busy helping my dad out with the ranch and she was too busy studying to become a genius. Or a nurse. Kind of the same thing. Knowing how smart Katy had been in school, I was relieved to find out she'd be helping Rowen in some capacity. Even if it was just to check a fluid bag.

"But I thought he was her husband." The dark-haired nurse crossed her arms, continuing to have a conversation that would suggest she didn't realize or care that I was in the room.

Katy's mouth drew into a tight line to keep from smiling as she stopped beside Rowen's bed. "Sperm donor."

I had to turn my head to hide my own smile. The disappointment on the two nurses' faces was so sudden and extreme, they looked like they'd just been told the cruise ship had left without them. I tried to wrap my head around how I wasn't off-limits as a married man, but I was apparently off-limits as a gay one. Couldn't really work that one out though.

After the nurses left, Katy stopped fighting her smile.

"You can thank me later."

"I thought ranch hands were bad when it came to things like professionalism and moral code . . ." I returned her smile to be polite, not because it came naturally. I wouldn't be able to give a genuine smile until Rowen was awake and no fewer than ten doctors had confirmed that she and the baby were stable and okay.

"Hospital staff . . ." Katy shook her head as her eyebrows lifted. "They can make truckers look like prep school girls. Shameless. And classless, as you just bore witness to. If they had mentioned that in nursing school, I might have considered a career change, but now I'm stuck. Go figure the girl whose idea of living it up is an extra scoop of ice cream picked the same career as a bunch of swingers whose idea of living it up requires a dictionary for me to understand."

I kept my smile in place. I remembered Katy being serious, almost severely so, and approaching life like it was a to-do list instead of an all-inclusive paid vacation. It didn't seem like much had changed.

"How have you been, Katy?" I noticed that she seemed to smile a bit easier now that we were alone.

"I had myself a double scoop last night at the Dairy Queen," she said as she finished adjusting Rowen's fluid bags. "I'm living it up."

I nodded. Her sense of humor had gotten a boost as well. "Good to hear."

"I'd ask you how you are, but since your wife's in here because she went into early labor and you look like you're two seconds away from losing your grip, I'll save that question for a different day." She moved to the head of Rowen's bed and starting pushing her out of the room.

"Had enough E.R. for one night?"

I popped out of my chair and followed her. "Had enough E.R. for one lifetime."

CHAPTER seven

Rowen

I WONDERED IF this was how Garth had felt when he'd first woken up in the hospital room in Wyoming. A brief moment of not having a clue what had happened or where you were while trying to pry your eyes open, only to remember a few seconds later exactly what had happened and where you were right when your eyes were up to the task of opening.

I was taking my time opening those eyes of mine. I needed to figure out what to say and how to look the second Jesse saw I was awake. He would be a wreck. He had a right to be a wreck. In my attempts to play off everything about my body, I'd put myself and, more importantly, the baby at risk. I couldn't take that chance again. I couldn't try to convince myself and everyone else that the pain I felt was indigestion or the light-headedness was from getting up too fast.

I'd taken it too far. Played with fire and gotten burned. I wouldn't do it again and risk being totally consumed by the fire next time.

I knew the baby was okay—I'd heard it's staccato heartbeat echoing around me before I'd heard my slower one thrumming in the background—but I didn't know what exactly had happened or what exactly would come next. That was what got me to finally open my eyes.

As expected, the first thing I saw was Jesse. His face was practically hovering above mine, his eyes lost and his expression matching. I tried to force a smile, but nothing came. I'd reached peak levels of bullshit a few faked smiles and assurances ago.

His hand moved to my face as he exhaled. "Welcome back." His thumb brushed down my cheek. His voice sounded weak, barely audible, but relief saturated those small-sounding words.

Moving took a little more effort than I would have liked, but when I managed to finally lift my hand high enough to cover his on my face, I said, "You say that like I wasn't actually expected to make it back . . . from wherever I went."

Instead of replying, he checked the monitors situated around my bed.

"What happened?"

He took a second to answer. "You went into early labor."

My heart rate monitor beeped faster, filling up the silent room.

"They stopped it. Everything's okay now," Jesse said quickly. "You're fine. The baby's fine. It's okay."

A tremble tingled down my back. I'd gone into labor early? Nearly three months early? As if we didn't have enough odds stacked against us in this pregnancy, we had to deal with pre-term labor too?

"Are you okay?" I asked, knowing the answer he'd give me would be different from the one on his face.

When he nodded, chunks of hair fell over his forehead and into his eyes. "I'm okay now."

My arm wrapped around my stomach. "Did I pass out or something? Is that why I don't remember anything from you bolting through the E.R. doors to right now?"

Jesse swallowed. "Yeah, your heart . . ." He swallowed again, his eyes drifting to a corner of the room. "Just the very start of you going into labor was too much for your heart. You weren't getting enough oxygen . . ."

My heart stopped. The malfunctioning thing actually stopped. I didn't say a word until it restarted. "If I wasn't getting enough oxygen, that means the baby wasn't—"

Jesse's head shook. "We made it here in time. Barely, but we made it. You and the baby are both safe. Healthy."

I didn't miss the subtle edge in his voice that suggested *For now.* That was when I felt it. The guilt. If I hadn't already been lying down, it would have knocked me over. I'd been feeling weird all day. I'd been feeling really weird all night. I'd written it off to indigestion and normal pregnancy woes so as not to freak my already freaked-out husband out even more and avoid him rushing me to the emergency room. Turned out, the emergency room was exactly what I needed. God, if we hadn't gotten there in time . . . if I had kept playing off that I was fine . . . if Garth hadn't driven so fast . . . if Jesse hadn't been so keyed in to my every move . . .

All of those dot, dot, dots led to the same place.

"Thank you," I whispered, telling myself I wouldn't cry. This time, I would come out the victor in my battle against hormones. I lost. Again. "Thank you for taking such good care of me." My hand skimmed up my stomach. "For taking such good care of *us*."

Some of the creases on his face softened, but they didn't disappear. They never disappeared completely anymore. "It's my job to take care of my family." His hand moved up my face, combing the hair back from my face. "I take that job seriously."

I was able to find a smile. "You take that job beyond seriously." Before he could open his mouth to defend himself, I added, "And I love that about you."

Something close to a laugh came from him. When he relaxed into the chair beside my bed, he fell into it like he hadn't slept for weeks. I knew for a fact the truth wasn't far from that. "Indigestion?"

I bit the inside of my cheek. "Apparently early labor and severe indigestion feel shockingly alike. Good to know, just in case, you know, this happens again . . ." This had better not happen again. I didn't think Jesse could take it. I wasn't sure if I could.

"Are you going to stop giving me the tough person routine now? Will you actually admit when you're not feeling good or something doesn't feel right?" His voice was soft, but his words hit me in the opposite way.

"I will never stop playing the tough person routine because that's what's gotten me through the hard parts in life and will continue to get me though them." My voice filled the room, and I found myself wondering if I was saying it more for my benefit or his. "The only way I'll make it through the next three months is by holding on to that tough grittiness you're obviously not a fan of." Just like that, I saw hurt bleed into his face. It was so easy to wound those we love most because they took their armor off around us. "I'm tough. That's who I am. Please don't ask me to be a lesser version of myself. I'd never ask you to do the same."

I watched him fumble to find the right words. I waited as his mind raced through what to say next. Finally, his face lowered to mine. Instead of answering with words, he answered with a kiss. And then another.

"You're right. I'm sorry," he said before kissing me one last time.

My flash of anger was extinguished as suddenly as if a water tower had just been dumped over it. "You're right too though. I'm also sorry." I wound my hand around the back of his neck and pulled him back to me until our foreheads touched. "I promise I will speak up when I'm not feeling right or something's bothering me. I can do that. I just don't think I can make it through this if I let myself get softer now. I need all of that crazy rough and tough thing you fell in love with now more than ever."

His eyes closed. Like that, he almost looked like the peaceful Jesse I remembered. The one I missed. "I know." His forehead creased against mine. "It's okay. Everything's going to be okay."

We stayed like that for an eternity. Or for a fleeting moment. Time got lost when we were like that because it just didn't matter. It became inconsequential.

Of course that would be when a certain person's voice echoed down the hospital hallway and interrupted our quiet moment.

"This place is a goddamned fucking circus!"

Jesse exhaled. I groaned.

"First they won't tell us anything in that joke of an emergency room, and now they won't tell us where they've moved her! I'll just keep searching each and every room on each and every floor of this hick hospital until I find them!"

I could make out Josie's voice in the background but not any of her specific words. Unlike her fiancé, she knew proper hospital etiquette wasn't screaming profanities and insults down the halls.

"You better go grab him before he gets himself into trouble," I said as Jesse stood.

"I guarantee he's already in trouble," Jesse said as he moved for the door.

"Okay, then before he gets hauled off in cuffs and spends the night of his engagement party curled up on a concrete slab beside a guy named Bubba."

He paused in the doorway. "For no other reason than I'd pay good money to see Garth in that kind of situation, I'm tempted to let him keep screaming his lungs out." When I gave him a disapproving look, Jesse raised his hands. "But since he's the reason we made it here in record-setting time, I'll save him from tallying up another mark on his record. Be right back."

He lingered in the doorway for a moment, looking at me like he was afraid I'd vanish if he left, then he made his way down the hall. From his boot-steps, I knew he was hustling. Not even half a minute later, Jesse was dragging Garth, who was dragging Josie, into the room.

"Found them," Jesse announced, seeming to sigh with relief when he found me exactly where he'd left me.

"This hospital is a—"

"Goddamn fucking circus?" I interrupted as I waved at Josie. "Yeah, the rest of the county heard your opinion on the place."

"Including our baby . . ." Jesse mumbled as he made his way back to the chair beside my bed.

Oops. I gave him an I'm really, really, *really* sorry look. I had been trying to watch my language. Good practice for when a toddler was running around and repeating every single word they heard. It was difficult, if not impossible, to keep up with that goal with Garth Black in the room though. He could bring out the profane in anyone.

"We need to get you transferred to a different hospital. I know more about the human anatomy than these clowns." Garth hitched his thumb over his shoulder, as if he was just waiting for the signal from me to roll me out of there.

"You know about more certain *parts* of the human anatomy—no argument from me there," I said.

A nurse appeared in my doorway, lifting a brow and a finger to her lips as she gave Garth The Look.

"Clowns!" he shouted.

"Quiet down please. Patients need their rest." The nurse didn't even sound perturbed. She must have been used to frazzled visitors shouting obscenities.

Garth snorted and stuck out his arm, ramrod straight and middle digit pointing to the sky. "How's this for quiet?" He waved it a few times before slamming the door closed. "Gets the same message across, I think."

"Thank you for alienating every single nurse on our floor, Black. Really appreciate it." Jesse scrubbed his face, looking exhausted. He looked older too. Older than he had at the start of the night. It was like every one of these adrenaline-fueled crises aged him a few years.

"How are you doing, Sterling-Walker? How's the little Sterling-Walker doing?" Garth's hand slipped into Josie's as they approached me. Concern was an emotion a person didn't normally see on Garth Black's face, yet it was the only thing there right now.

"We're good. We're both good." I scooted over to make room for Garth and Josie to sit on the edge of the bed. Josie was the only one who did; Garth chose to pace at the foot of my bed. "Thank you guys for getting us here so quickly, and I'm so sorry this happened in the middle of your engagement party. You guys should head back. Enjoy what's left of a great night."

Garth slid up behind Josie and dropped his arms around her. "I'm here with my three best friends in the whole world. This *is* a great night."

"The atmosphere leaves a bit to be desired though," I said. From the smells to the sounds to the sights, there was nothing inviting or warm about a hospital room.

Garth scanned the room. "True enough. So why don't we bust you out of here, now that you're all stable and shit, and go finish the night some place else? Anywhere else," he added when a grumpy-faced nurse shoved open the door and marched in.

A less grumpy-faced doctor followed her. The nurse shooed Josie and Garth away from my bed, but no amount of shooing worked with Jesse. He stayed right at the head of my bed, arms crossed, jaw locked.

The doctor introduced himself and the nurse, but I didn't catch their names, probably because the doctor mumbled. Jesse shifted as the doctor and nurse scanned the beeping machines scattered around me.

Garth waved his finger between the two and mouthed, "Are these clowns for real?"

I shook my head. "Control yourself," I mouthed back. "When can I leave?" I asked the doctor, who was still studying one of the machines.

His brows pinched together. "Providing you and the baby are both still stable in the morning, I see no reason why you won't be discharged tomorrow."

I had to lean in and watch his lips to catch most of what he was saying, but I exhaled with relief. "Thank God. No offense, but hospitals make me uncomfortable."

"Really?" the nurse chimed in as she changed one of my I.V. bags. "Most people feel all kinds of warm fuzzies in a hospital."

Jesse's brows hit the ceiling. I grabbed his wrist and gave it a squeeze before he could open his mouth. No doubt she was one of the nurses Garth had spread his "charm" around with.

"Will I need to take any extra precautions?" I asked the doctor, ignoring the increasingly grumpy nurse. Her attitude might have had something to do with Garth making vulgar hand motions in her direction. "You know, get extra rest, no more spicy food, limit the time on my feet? That kind of thing?"

The doctor finally looked at me. From his expression, he was waiting for something to dawn on me or for me to catch the punchline. Jesse sighed. Great, so he knew something I didn't. Based on the looks on both Jesse's and the doctor's faces, it wouldn't be something I'd be thrilled to learn about.

"To answer your question, yes, you will need to take extra precautions going forward unless you want to go into early labor again." The doctor's gaze scanned the length of the bed. "You'll need to be on bed rest for the duration of your pregnancy."

The machine beeping my heartbeat skipped a few beats. "And, like, by bed rest you mean . . ." I told myself to stay calm. “A few hours in the afternoon to lie down and rest?”

The doctor came close to smiling. Then he shook his head. “I mean unless you’re on your way to or from the toilet, you’re in bed.”

Another silent stretch from my heart rate monitor. “Oh, so when you say bed rest, what you really mean is a rare, especially brutal form of torture.”

CHAPTER eight

Rowen

I'D BEEN OFF when I blamed the doctor for dishing out bed rest. Wrong in the sense of labeling it a rare, brutal form of torture. No, what bed rest was . . . it went beyond that. Having to lay in bed, day in and day out, sunrise to sunset, sunset to sunrise, over and over and *over* again. If it hadn't already driven me there, I felt like I was mere days away from getting dropped off at Platform Insane.

Jesse, along with the rest of the Walkers, had been a saint through it all, but I'd been the opposite of a saint for the past two months. I only had one more month to go, but how was I supposed to make it another thirty days when I wasn't sure I could get through tomorrow?

That was when I felt the kick. When I saw it too. As was typical, whenever I felt doom and gloom about the whole bed rest situation, someone reminded me why I was doing it. This doom and gloom moment's someone was the growing baby in my stomach. Nothing like a not-so-gentle kick to the belly button to remind me why I was, for once in my life, being a good patient and following the doctor's orders: for the baby. To keep it safe and give it time to get stronger before it came into the world. The kid encouraged me almost as much as the Walkers did—its positive, uplifting tendency was very much like that side of the family. It definitely didn't get those traits from my side.

I'd fallen asleep for my third nap of the morning—if I watched any more morning television, I would throw the remote through the screen, right between the eyes of that perma-smile, perky blond host—but from the looks of the clock perched on the table beside my bed, my nap had barely registered at the fifteen-minute mark. That seemed to be becoming a habit. The further along in my pregnancy I got, the shorter my naps and stretches of sleep became.

My day pretty much consisted of the excitement level of a senior citizen in a retirement community, minus the outings to the grocery store and senior center for bingo. I woke up before the sun was up, which really blew since I'd never been an early riser. Of course, when I would have preferred to sleep eighteen hours a night, my body was only up to the task of a solid six. I staggered to the bathroom, assisted by my faithful husband, did my business, then staggered back to bed to try and fail to fall asleep for another three hours. Usually that resulted in me giving up with a grand sigh and a few punches to the bed. I floundered through my pile of "entertainment" on my bedside table for the remote and fired up the TV only to scan the channels and find that America's issues don't stem from entitled youth but from suck-ass television choices.

After that depressing reminder every morning, I turned off the television, resisted the urge to fling the remote across the room, and tried to fall asleep again. By that point, Jesse'd been up and working for close to five hours and usually came back to check on me at his parents' place. The Walkers had been generous enough to sacrifice their living room to my bed-rest sentence.

Mrs. Walker had said it was the best option since it was so close to the downstairs bathroom, large enough that everyone could fit inside so we could all have dinners together, and the abundant windows let in plenty of sunshine in the morning and the smell of late summer flowers in the afternoon. I didn't want to sequester their living room. I already felt like enough of a burden being unable to do anything but ring my bell when I needed something, but Rose had insisted. Neil had insisted. Jesse had insisted. Pretty much everyone but me had insisted. So the living room it was. My bedroom. The place where I spent twenty-three hours of my day. The other hour I lived it up in the bathroom.

I heard Old Bessie coming—one of the perks of having a husband who drove a beast that had rolled off the assembly line when our grandparents had been teenagers—and remembered what I'd been doing before taking my power (third) nap of the morning.

I had time to organize my desk table and my sheets and hair so I didn't look half-rabid before I heard Jesse's boot-steps bounding up the front porch. Rose and the girls were in town visiting the farmer's market and stopping at a couple of stores, so the house had been especially quiet. So much so, the fridge had started to sound deafening.

As much as I hated that Jesse took extra time out of his day to drive back here from wherever he'd been working —he was so busy he, unlike me, barely had time to take a bathroom break—I looked forward to this time of the day like a five-year-old waiting for Christmas morning.

It was just past ten, which meant I'd been bored out

of my mind for a few hours since waking up and was just about at my breaking point when he made it back to have his lunch with me. I'd never told him how nuts the bed rest thing was driving me, but I supposed all he had to do was look in my eyes. They gave it all away. After that first week, he started coming back to the house to have lunch with me, and he hadn't missed a day since. Even if his sisters and mom were home to keep me company—or more accurately, keep me from shaving my head and listening to Joss Stone on repeat—he still came back.

He opened the front door quietly, not letting the screen door slam shut. He always did that just in case I was asleep. I never was though. I never slept during the ten o'clock hour because that was Jesse's and my time. One of the best hours of my day, if not *the* best.

After that, I knew he was pausing in the hall to slide out of his boots so they wouldn't make any noise on the hardwood floors, so I spoke up. "I'm awake. No need to un-layer. Unless you're planning on un-layering everything."

Yeah, right. That part of our married life had gone from "outlook sketchy" to "grab a duster and sweep the cobwebs away." This time it was doctor's orders, not just a paranoid husband's precautions, so I had another month to endure of not getting laid by my oh-so-lay-worthy husband. I was positively rolling in a bed of win and yippee these days.

Jesse moved inside the living room, his smile moving into place when he saw me. I was eight and a half months pregnant, hadn't been able to do anything more than be a drag for two months, and he still smiled at me like I was the girl he'd fallen in love with several summers ago.

Okay, so not all parts of my life sucked.

"Why would you be asleep when that's what you're supposed to be doing on bed rest, right?"

I motioned at the bed I'd been having fantasies of torching in a giant bonfire when this whole thing was over. "In order to sleep, a person has to be tired. In order to be tired, a person has to have done something more than turn from one side to the other in bed. 'Bed rest' is the biggest oxymoron out there."

Something flashed in his eyes. "Then this is probably the perfect time to distract you with a present?"

"I know I should be all selfless and say, 'You didn't have to do that' or 'I don't need any other gift than getting to spend time with you' but"—I lifted onto my elbows and winked—"Gimme, gimme."

He laughed as he ducked back into the hallway and out onto the porch, but this time he let the screen door slam shut. It whined open only a few seconds later, and a few more after that, he came back into view. Or at least partly came back into view. Half of him was hidden behind the large object he seemed to be part wrestling and part balancing in his arms.

My heart thumped harder in my chest. "Is that what I think it is?"

"What do you think it is?"

"Something to get our freak on with." I suppressed my smile when Jesse broke to a momentary halt.

With a clearing of his throat, he continued toward the little table that rolled across my bed so I could eat my meals, try and fail to sketch something, or bang my head against when the urge arose. Which was often.

"You're worse than a teenage boy," he said, setting

what was in his arms on my roller table.

"That's because, unlike the majority of teen boys pretending they know all about sex, I actually have had it, frequently, and enjoyed it just as frequently. I know what I'm missing out on, thus giving me the right to whine, complain, and be unable to carry on a conversation without referring to it in a direct or indirect sense."

Jesse smiled as he worked on positioning his masterpiece on the table. "I can't argue with that." He tightened a few clamps around the lip of the table, securing the object in place. "Do you have any *other* guesses? Ones that don't involve us utilizing it to 'get our freak on'?"

The words sounded so wrong coming from Jesse's mouth, I came close to laughing, but I was too excited about what he was rolling in front of me. "It's an easel," I whispered, my tone as reverent as it got. "An easel for a bed jockey whose muscles are about to jellify and whose brains already have."

Jesse rolled the table a bit toward the foot of my bed since my stomach was in the way, then he grabbed an armful of pillows from the couch before stacking them behind my back. "Also known as an easel for a woman on bed rest."

"Wait, you made this?" As Jesse propped me up a bit higher with the mountain of pillows, I noticed the details and craftsmanship that had gone into making the easel. I'd owned enough easels in my day to recognize a store-bought one from a handmade one.

"Well, yeah. Do you think it will work okay? I wasn't sure . . ." He rubbed at the back of his neck as he fiddled with a few of the clamps, adjusting them a bit tighter. "I took a look at your easels when I was packing up the condo and tried to get this one close, but I wasn't sure . . ."

I grabbed his hand, which was still fussing with the clamps. "It's perfect. So much so, I kind of want to cry, and you know how much I hate to cry."

He stopped playing with the easel with his other hand too. "I thought you could use a distraction from all of this. Sorry it took so long for me to finish." He sat on the edge of my bed, his arm circling my stomach like it was instinctive. "I started it the first week you were put on bed rest and I meant to finish it in a few days . . . but that didn't happen."

I couldn't stop grinning at the easel. He couldn't have given me a more perfect gift at this point in time, not even if he'd booked me a daily massage. This right here meant I'd be able to draw from the right kind of angle or paint even. I could entertain myself for hours so long as I had a pencil or a brush or hell, even a crayon. Trying to create something with a notepad balanced on my stomach or lying flat on the table didn't work. But this would.

Screw the close to crying. When I blinked, a tear spilled down my cheek, and I didn't care enough to wipe it away. If ever there was a reason to cry, it was over something like this.

"Please don't feel bad." I rubbed at the creases in his forehead, trying to erase them. "This is one of the best presents I've ever gotten. You have no idea how many sessions of therapy you've saved me with this thing. No idea."

"You like it? Do you think it will work okay?" His forehead started to smooth out.

"Heck, yeah, times two."

I reached for a notebook to tear out a sheet of paper,

but Jesse got to it first and clipped it into place on the easel. He handed me a graphite pencil right after that. I raised the pencil to the paper and drew a few quick lines, then a few more, and before I knew it, my hand was flying across the paper like it had been starved of sustenance for months. I didn't know what I was drawing, but it didn't matter. It just felt good to create something again. Jesse stayed silent beside me, going from watching my face to the sheet of paper.

"God, Jesse, this thing is, like, so perfect. The angle is just right, and the height is spot-on. I couldn't have designed this better if I'd tried." Even when I glanced away from the paper long enough to look at him, my hand kept moving.

"Well now I'm really sorry I didn't finish this sooner."

"It's not like you've been busy or anything, right?" I kept smiling. I felt like it was plastered to my face and would be impossible to remove. "It's not like you've been packing up our condo back in Seattle, getting it cleaned, and listing it for sale. And it's not like you've been laying the foundation and framing our house a mile down the road. And it's not like you've been helping your dad out around the ranch and helping Garth over at his place. You haven't been busy the last couple of months *at all*. I can't imagine why you didn't finish this easel in record time."

He rubbed at the back of his neck and raised a shoulder. "I'm used to being busy."

"Busy is one thing. What you've taken on is three full-time jobs."

"It's not so bad." Another shoulder raise.

My hand paused, tipped against the easel. "Other than

the few hours you squeeze in for sleep and these few minutes during lunch when you sneak back here to see me, you haven't stopped moving since we came to Montana." I swallowed. The shadows under his eyes seemed extra noticeable in the late morning light spilling through the window. "I'm worried about you."

Half of his mouth curled up. "You're the pregnant one on bed rest with a heart condition, and you're worried about me?"

"I'm not the one trying to be everything to everyone all the time, so yes, I am worried about you," I said, tightening my fingers through his. "You might be the one with a healthy heart, but it won't stay healthy if you don't take a break soon."

He shook his head, but I knew he recognized the truth in what I was saying. A person couldn't carry on the way he had without starting to feel like they were more toeing the line of death than life. I admired his work ethic and I respected that he wouldn't know how to complain if someone ordered him to, but I was worried. If he didn't back off and give his head and body some real rest, I was terrified it would be his heart that would give out instead of mine.

"I'll be fine." His eyes didn't meet mine when he answered.

"Hey, I know that answer. I invented it. Don't B.S. a B.S.'er." I arched an eyebrow at him to make sure he'd noticed my substitute for the foul language he was worried about exposing our child to in the womb.

He acknowledged my efforts with a gentle squeeze of his hand. "Are you fine?"

"I'm better than fine. I'm fantastic. For real this

time." I motioned at my easel and him. "How could I not be?"

"Then I'm fantastic too." He kissed the tip of my nose. "I'll let you get back to your sketch."

"You just got here."

"Garth's meeting me over at our place to help me with the rafters in fifteen minutes. I promised I'd help him move their new washer and dryer into their place when we were done." He kissed me again, but this time it was on the lips.

"So does that mean I'll see you at about the usual time tonight? Eight?"

"Maybe nine."

"Jesse, you can't keep doing this. You're going to keel over dead one day, and how's our child going to grow up to be a well-adjusted person with just me as a parent? I need you to keep our kid from becoming a totally pessimistic too-strange-for-their-own-good person. I need the goodness and sunny disposition you'll bring to the parenting potpourri."

My spiel got him to smile, but it didn't stop him from continuing out of the room. "I'll be there, every step of the way. Just make sure you're with me too."

"Does that mean you'll be home before everyone's gone to bed for the night?"

"It means I'll try." He paused when he got to the hallway. "Hey, you want me to make you a sandwich or something for lunch before I head out? I think Mom just restocked our peanut butter stores . . ."

My shoulders fell. I was doing nothing more constructive than comparing the number of freckles on my right forearm and my left—my right had two more than my left—while he was out busting his ass trying to build a life for our family. Why was he the one offering to make me lunch when I should have at least been capable of slapping a few pieces of meat and cheese between a couple slices of bread for him? Oh yeah, because I wasn't supposed to be on my feet all of five minutes to make my husband a lunch.

"From the time I've had breakfast, I've burned a whole eleven calories. I think I'm good. But thanks." I pointed my pencil at him. "But this is your lunch hour, slash lunch *minute*, so maybe you should eat a few thousand calories to replace those you used up helping your dad with the fences this morning."

His jeans, which had once been a miracle of science they'd fit so snugly, had become loose around his hips and, sigh, his backside. If he lost any more weight by forgetting to eat like he had been, those jeans would fall off of him.

"I'm not hungry, but if that changes, I've got a banana and granola bar in Old Bessie."

"Wow. A whole banana and granola bar. You could go on for weeks with that."

His eyes lifted to the ceiling. "I'm not hungry."

"But that doesn't mean your body doesn't need food."

He gave up with a sigh. "Fine. I'll grab one of the sandwiches Mom left in the fridge. Will that make you happy?"

"Only if you follow up grabbing that sandwich with *eating* that sandwich."

"I promise," he said.

"I love you, Jesse," I called before he disappeared from view. "Even more than I love this easel you made me, and I love this easel a lot. Like, so much I'm not sure it's healthy to be in love with an inanimate object to the extent I am with this thing."

His soft chuckle echoed in the hall. "I love you too, Rowen. More than any animate or inanimate object in the whole world."

When I heard the screen door whine open, I yelled, "Your sandwich!"

"Sorry. I forgot."

I could tell by his tone that he really had. Not even five seconds had passed, and the sandwich had slipped his mind. As if I needed to worry any more for him, I felt it grow right then, crashing over all of the former in typhoon-like waves that wouldn't end. He couldn't keep running himself ragged. He was going to burn out or worse . . .

After I heard the creak of the fridge door, followed by his boot-steps jogging through the kitchen, he stuck his head back in the living room. "Love you." He gave a quick wave, the sandwich in his hand.

"Eat that sandwich and prove it."

He peeled the plastic baggie back, smiled at me, then sank his teeth into the sandwich.

CHAPTER nine

Jesse

I FINISHED THE sandwich. Truer story—I inhaled the sandwich. I hadn't realized I'd been hungry until I tore into the first bite to prove my love—because what better way is there to prove you love someone than by eating a ham and cheese sandwich, right? But after the first bite, my stomach growled so loudly, I heard it even over the roar of Old Bessie's engine thundering to life.

After finishing the sandwich in a whole three more bites, I found myself wishing I'd grabbed a couple more. I couldn't really remember the last thing I'd eaten—I had to have thrown something down at breakfast that morning, right?—but my body, and stomach mainly, was making it rather clear it was starving.

I was tempted to make a detour into town to grab a bag of burgers and fries from the old drive-thru, but I was already running late. If Garth beat me to the house, he would start working without me, and I didn't want to worry about him breaking his back moving around rafters. Breaking it once was enough for any one person.

The spot where Rowen and I had decided to build our

home had been one of my favorite places since I'd been a boy. It was tucked down in a wide valley that a creek ran through in the spring and early summer. By the time August rolled around, the creek was nothing more than a place to go have mud fights with friends, but it was a great place to cool off at earlier in the summer, and it made the most beautiful sound trickling around the rocks and shrubs and grass lining the creek.

We'd originally planned to build the house right beside the creek so we could open up our windows at night and let the sound of that lazily moving water put us to sleep for those four months out of the year it ran. Then Rowen mentioned how much our little boy—she was still positive we were having a boy—would love to play in it. She said we'd have to be on the lookout for plastic boats to float down it and little buckets and shovels to make mud pies with.

Where she'd seen a playground for our child, I'd seen something else: a potentially deadly landmine. A creek? Running water? What had I been thinking of, building a house where we wanted to raise a family so close to a body of water I couldn't put a gate around or a cover on? Sure, it might not have run much deeper than knee level at its deepest, but a child could drown in mere inches of water. I'd heard a story like that on the news. I couldn't build our house ten yards back from a threat like that creek. A toddler could climb out of his or her bed at night, sneak through a front door to go splash around in the water, and drown when they slipped on a rock and knocked themselves unconscious. What had I been thinking?

I didn't tell Rowen the reason I'd insisted we move the house farther back from the creek—a mere four hundred yards—but I guessed she knew I had reasons other than not wanting the skunks and marmots and other animals that would head to the creek for a drink to make a home beneath our front porch or inside of our shed. She let me have my paranoia when it came to keeping her and the baby safe, and I figured she was so calm because she assumed it would pass after she'd safely delivered the baby and both she and it were okay. I hoped that too.

But I couldn't be sure. How could a person be less paranoid when it came to taking precautions with the people they cared for most in the world? How did someone mitigate their risks when it came to their family? How did a father "let go" when it came to things like handing over the car keys to his sixteen-year-old? I didn't know. But I hoped I'd learn.

The "road" leading to our house was more of an I-think-this-is-the-way kind of trail that had become more pronounced over the past couple of months with the regular traffic between Garth's, mine, and my dad's trucks. The soil wasn't too rocky, so the drive wasn't too bumpy, which Rowen would appreciate after bouncing down so many back roads she said her teeth chattered permanently now.

Garth must have just beaten me to the site because he was jumping out of his truck when it came into view. The house wouldn't be a particularly large or fancy—a one-floor rancher with three bedrooms, two bathrooms, and a dining room big enough to hold all of our friends and family relatively comfortably at Thanksgiving or insert other holiday dinner here. Coming in at just under two thousand square feet and designed with the ideal balance of economical and quality, I couldn't help but feel like I was looking at one of those sprawling mansions overlooking Lake Washington in Seattle. Nothing more than the foundation and framework was complete, but an overwhelming sense of pride took me over every time I drove up to it. This was where my family would live. This was where my kids would grow up. This was where I would spend winter nights curled up beneath a pile of blankets with my wife and summer ones running ice-cold glasses of lemonade across each other's foreheads while rocking on the porch swing.

This was home.

It was a good feeling. The home I'd known as a boy had stopped feeling quite so home-like when Rowen and I got married, as I supposed it would for anyone leaving the family they grew up with to join the family they would grow old with. The apartment and then the condo in Seattle had never really felt like home, at least not unless Rowen and I were together. I'd spent nights in one-and-a-half star hotels when we'd traveled to watch Black rodeo a few times, and even in those, when I'd wind my body around her in bed, I was home.

This place though, it already felt like home, even when it was just me out here, pounding countless nails into countless two-by-fours. Or even when an old friend was waving his middle finger instead of the rest of his hand as I pulled up beside his truck.

"Nice of you to show up, Jess!" he hollered before I'd turned off Old Bessie's engine. "It's not like I've got important things to do with my time or anything!"

Snagging my tool belt from the passenger seat, I threw open my door and crawled out. "You showed up a whole minute before I did. Sorry to keep you waiting for sixty seconds. I didn't realize how precious time was to the man who could waste entire weekends drinking cheap whiskey in a busted lawn chair."

Garth finished cinching his tool belt before grabbing a couple of yellow paper bags from his truck, followed by a cardboard tray holding two massive Styrofoam cups with the familiar QuikStop Drive-Thru logo stamped on them. "Those are the old days, Jess, the days of the past. I take my time much more seriously now."

"Good to know." When I cinched my own tool belt into place, I found it hung too far down on my hips. Frowning, I had to move it down two additional notches to get it to fit properly.

"I mean, do you know what I could do with sixty seconds?" he continued, traipsing over to the porch.

"Count to ten?" I smiled at the ground when a French fry flew my way and slapped me in the chest.

"Be in and out of the arena, earning another championship buckle, polish the chrome door handles on my sweet ass truck, polish something else—"

"You're talking about silverware, right? Because I've told you before, and I don't want to tell you again, that I'm uncomfortable having conversations with you circling around polishing and human anatomy. Take that up with Josie. She's the one who said yes to spending the rest of her life with you. The rest of us are more contingent on your behavior."

"Good to know I've got good friends," Garth jeered as he sat on the edge of the porch before shaking the yellow paper bags at me. "Especially when I ordered the Family Round-Up combo at your favorite burger joint in town."

"Other than the M-word burger joint, and I use the word burger in the loosest is-this-really-meat? sense, QuikStop is the *only* burger joint in town." I could smell the grease from here, and it made my stomach growl. That ham and cheese sandwich must have been like nudging a hibernating bear. Now that it was waking up, it was ravenous and intent upon eating everything in sight.

"Do you want a Whoopie burger and double fry or not?" Garth waved one of the giant burgers wrapped in yellow paper. Grease had already seeped a wide ring around the paper, and the special sauce was oozing out of the corners. "Because I ordered you five. Three for now, two for a snack later, along with a few orders of fries and a colossal-sized summer strawberry milkshake." Garth tapped one of the true-to-size Styrofoam cups, glaring at the one leaking a few rivers of pink cream down the side. "Do you know how it feels rolling up to a drive-thru window in my badass truck, with my badass name, and order a summer strawberry shake? I mean, dammit, Jess, I've got a reputation to uphold."

I made sure the volume on my phone was as high up as it would go so I wouldn't miss a call from Rowen and shoved it deep into my back pocket. "I didn't ask you to order me a summer strawberry milkshake, or enough grease and sodium to give a dozen men cardiac arrest, so don't take your reputation-upholding issues out on me."

Garth aimed a tight smile in my direction before tossing one of the yellow bags at me. I caught it. Barely. "Yeah, yeah. Enough with the chatter. Eat already before you wake up next week and discover there're no more notches to go down on that tool belt."

Ah, now I got why he'd gone all gluttonous at the

QuikStop. “Why is everyone so concerned with trying to fatten me up?”

When I opened the bag, I found he really had ordered me five burgers. The fries weren’t inside, but that was only because there wasn’t any room to fit anything else. Two and a half pounds of beef, paired with just as much weight in toppings and buns, could really fill a drive-thru bag.

“Because you’re size Manorexic.” Garth waved a French fry at me before popping it into his mouth. “I mean, Christ, I can practically count your ribs through that shirt of yours.”

I knew better, but I still glanced down to check. I was in my standard white tee, same brand and size as I’d worn for the past five years, but now that I was actually paying attention, it did seem a bit looser. It didn’t quite pull around the chest like it had, and more material floated above my belt than ever had before. I hadn’t been on a scale in over a year, since my last physical, but I guessed I’d lost some weight. “So I’ve lost a few L.B.s—big deal. I’d like to see how you fare when Josie is carrying you two’s first child.”

Garth was in the middle of peeling his wrapper back from his burger. He stopped long enough to give me a look that led me to believe he thought I was mental. “A *few* pounds? Yeah, right. And I’ve got a shot at entering through Heaven’s Gates when I kick the bucket.”

I kicked the toe of his boot before settling down on the porch beside him and reaching into the fry bag. They were still warm. Starting to get a little soggy from the grease they were swimming in, but still warm and wonderfully salty. I felt the granules rolling between the pads of my fingers. “Fine. So you’re on the Fatten Jesse Up bandwagon now too. I guess you're in good company since it seems like everyone in my life is doing the same thing." I tossed a few fries into my mouth and found they were every bit as good soggy as they were fresh from the fryer. At that point, my stomach wasn't discerning about texture so long as the grease and salt packed a punch.

"Hey, I'm not trying to fatten you up," Garth said around a mouthful of burger. "I'm trying to keep you from becoming a skeleton with skin."

I washed down another handful of fries with a drink of milkshake. They were the old-fashioned kind, made with real ice cream, so a person felt like they would pass out from trying to get the first bit of milkshake up the straw and into their mouth. Somehow, all of the effort made the shake taste that much better.

"You know, I've always been more of a fan of silence when I eat. How about you?" I unwrapped one of my five burgers while Garth tore into the rest of his.

"I'll shut up if you eat, how 'bout that?" he said before going to work on his own colossal milkshake.

I didn't hide my smirk when I noticed the pink liquid dotted with red flecks of strawberry finally making its way up his straw. "What about that pristine reputation of yours?"

Garth shot me a glare but kept working at his shake. "Summer strawberry is the shit," he said around his straw. "Shut up and eat already, Skelator."

IT WAS A good thing I'd forced myself to down all of one burger, most of an order of fries, and half of that milkshake. After the day Garth and I'd spent raising the roof, literally, I needed all of the energy I had. I'd spent plenty of hard days doing manual labor, but today's check-list had me wishing I kept a bottle of pain relievers in my truck. I'd have been reaching for it right about now.

Like me, Garth was trying to disguise the fact that we were so bushed we would have been content to crawl into the beds of our trucks and fall asleep. However, the day wasn't done. Working on the roof had taken a couple more hours than expected, but Garth didn't know how to quit a job that wasn't complete any better than I did. So we stayed and finished what we'd started. We each downed another burger and what was left of the cold fries on the porch before packing up and heading for Garth's place.

He told me to head home and get some sleep—that his washer and dryer could wait until tomorrow—but I couldn't do that. He'd busted his ass for the past ten hours with me at my place; I could give him an hour of my time.

From Rowen's and my place, Garth and Josie's was only about a thirty-minute drive. But barely ten minutes into the drive, I felt my eyes burning with exhaustion right before my eyelids seemed to grow a mind of their own. They kept wanting to close and stay that way. I'd never come close to falling asleep at the wheel, not even during all of my journeys back and forth from Montana to Seattle, and some of those journeys were made late in the night. Sure, I'd been tired and bordering on exhausted, but I'd never felt like this—like the act of falling asleep wasn't voluntary. Like my body would betray itself and fall asleep on its own. That scared me. I'd driven past a small handful of wrecks that had been caused by the driver falling asleep at the wheel. Back then, it had always seemed so far-fetched that I could ever fall asleep while powering down a highway, but right now, feeling as if an elephant were pressing down on my eyelids, it seemed far too likely a reality.

I rolled down the window, stuck my head out, and sucked in a few deep breaths of cooling summer air. I should have known better. On my third breath, a bug kamikazed into my mouth and was swallowed before I could spit it out. After that, no one could accuse me of not getting my protein.

I kept the window down but stuck my head back inside. I proceeded to turn on some Cash. Well, I blasted Cash to the point that Old Bessie's speakers were rattling and sounded about to explode. With a few violent shakes of my head, just as many neck cracks, and twice as many bounces in my seat, I made it. Garth and Josie's place might have looked more blurry than clear and my head was swimming like I'd spent the day drinking instead of working, but I'd arrived in one awake piece.

When he crawled out of his truck, Garth looked almost as beat as I felt. He never just *crawled* out of his truck. He leapt, jumped, leaped, or peacocked out of his truck, kind of the way he did everything else.

"It's hell getting old, Jess," Garth called as I tried to peel myself out of my own truck without appearing as though every muscle in my body had been ripped to shreds.

"Can you imagine how much hell it'll be when we're actually old?" I replied as I approached the front steps.

Garth's nose curled. "Shit, why the hell did I pick ranching as my chosen career? If I had been smart, I'd have gotten into something where I could sit at a desk all day."

"I think desk jobs just mean getting different kinds of body aches."

"Yeah, plus, can you imagine me in a suit and tie?" Garth kicked his boots against the bottom step of the porch, sending chunks of dried mud and pieces of dried grass to the ground.

"No," I said, doing the same to my boots. Their place was still in sorry straits, but Josie treated it like a pristine country club. Mud and dirt was not allowed. "No, I cannot."

"So much for paying for delivery, right?" Garth nodded at the washer and dryer on the porch. "'Actually, sir, delivery just includes to the front door. Delivery and Install includes bringing the appliances inside and installing them,'" Garth rattled off in a high-pitched voice. "Small print sons of bitches."

"And you mean you, with all of your charm, couldn't coax them into making an exception?" I shook my head, knowing that when those delivery drivers had left yesterday, their impression of Garth Black was the opposite of charming.

"Yeah, well at least I'll know for next time that delivery means half-ass."

Garth and I moved to the washer first. We were both of the mindset that you start with the hardest-slash-heaviest task first.

"Thanks for the tip. Since I'll be needing to order only a half dozen appliances soon."

"Make sure you pay the extra for delivery and *installation* though, because I'm sure as shit not going to help you haul a double fridge into that place of yours." Garth grinned across the washer at me as we crouched into position to get a good hold on it.

"It's good to have good friends," I repeated his words before we heaved the washer up and moved it.

Josie had already thrown open the door, and she directed us down the hall and into the laundry room like she was bringing in a 747 from the runway. "Looking good, looking good. Nice and easy." She flagged us over to the wall where the washer and dryer were going. "Garth, your side is off balance. Jesse, you look like you're going to pass out. Please don't do it before you get my washer safely into place."

I shot her a smirk before letting out an exaggerated yawn. "About to pass out any moment is how I look all the time, Josie. Don't worry. Your washer is safe with me." And it was. It felt as heavy as if we were trying to move Garth's truck down a football field, but we managed it. Something about being exhausted all of the time meant my strength had been diminished by half lately.

"Dryer?" Garth panted at me once we'd moved the washer into position.

Garth had said he'd work on getting everything hooked up tomorrow, and I was relieved. I wasn't sure I'd make it through hauling the dryer in, let alone hanging around to finish hooking up two appliances I didn't have any experience installing. My mental fortitude was gone, out the door, totally useless when it came to reading instructions or figuring out what two plus two times two equaled.

By the time we'd made the second trip with the dryer, my heart felt as though it would explode from the day's efforts and from what felt like all of those sleepless nights coming to one sum total of unparalleled exhaustion. After scooting the dryer into position, I sat on the ground and leaned against the dryer to catch my breath. I planned on resting for a few seconds before taking off, but my eyelids finally won that war I'd been battling for the past hour.

I wasn't sure how long I'd been passed out when my phone went off, but from the feel of my shoulders and neck, it was longer than it should have been. "Hey, Rowen." My voice sounded like I'd been sleeping for a week instead of a half hour. "Sorry I'm so late. Things ran late at our place, and I think I just fell asleep against Garth and Josie's new dryer." I blinked a few times to clear my eyes and found a blanket had been tossed over my lap and a pillow was on either side of me—to either keep me from tipping over or to catch my head if I did, I wasn't sure.

"You sound beyond exhausted, Jesse," she said, sounding almost as tired. "I don't want you crawling into your truck and driving like that. Why don't you see if Garth and Josie will let you spend the night, okay? If you need the leverage, tell Garth he'll owe us when he sees what I've picked out for his bride's bedtime wear."

I chuckled, but it was all throaty with sleep. "No, I want to come home to you. I want to see you. I'll be fine. Really. I feel better already with that cat nap."

I didn't. I somehow felt worse, but I couldn't tell her that. What got me through these long days was the promise of crawling into bed with her at the end of them. She was my quiet, peaceful refuge, and even though I spent more nights awake than I did asleep, I always rolled out of bed the next morning feeling recharged.

"Stay. Sleep. For me."

I couldn't argue with her. I didn't have the energy, so instead I forced myself up from the ground and said, "I'll see you soon. Love you."

Her reply was a long sigh, but with a quick, "Love you back," she hung up. Like me, I think Rowen looked forward to our nights together as the only thing that got her through long days trapped in bed.

When I made my way down the hall, I found Garth and Josie camped out at their small kitchen table, eating what looked to be dinner at ten o'clock at night. Garth was more trying not to fall asleep between bites of steak, and Josie was picking at her green beans like she was more interested in making a pattern than actually eating them.

"Hey, sorry about going out like that," I said, stretching my arms in an attempt to get the blood pumping. "I can confidently say that your dryer is not the most ideal of places to fall asleep if you're looking to avoid debilitating neck pain."

Josie dropped her fork, and Garth stopped chewing the bite he'd been working on since I'd walked in.

"Please don't tell me you're planning on actually driving ten miles in your current condition," Josie said, grabbing the empty third plate at the table and moving toward the counter.

"I really am." I shook my head when I noticed her preparing another plate of food. "Thank you so much, Josie, but I'm not hungry. Your fiancé already clogged my arteries with five pounds of grease, so I'll be good until next year. Thank you though."

She threw a hand on her hip, plate still in hand. "You need to eat."

"No, I need to get home to my wife and then fall asleep."

"That's exactly the same thing I told her I needed

when she loaded up my plate and ordered me to eat." Garth scraped his fork across his plate, shuffling potatoes and beans around in an effort to look as though he'd eaten some. "But I'm too beat to even fuck, so I sure as hell am too tired to eat. I'll keep this force-feeding torture in mind for the next time I order you to eat a bagful of QuikStop burgers and fries, okay, Jess?"

I smiled through the cloud of exhaustion. Josie's glare and hand-on-hip angle twisted Garth's way.

"Deal," I said, waving at them before heading for the door.

"No way. Not so fast, Jesse Walker." Josie's voice followed me down the hall. She bounded up, Thermos in hand, right as I was about to open the door. "Coffee. Drink this." She shook her head when I took the Thermos, thanking her with a smile. "Damn fools. The both of you." She raised her voice to ensure a certain someone, who was probably asleep in his steak, could hear in the kitchen.

"Thanks for the coffee. Have a good night." I headed out the door and toward my truck.

"Say hi to Rowen for me, okay? Oh, and would you ask her if she'd rather have pink and blue cupcakes for the baby shower, or if green and yellow would be more appropriate? I can't decide, and since you two are the ones intent on torturing all of us planning a baby shower and wanting to buy gifts for a gender to-be-determined baby, I'll leave the cupcake-color decision in her court," Josie continued as I stumbled up to Old Bessie. I did a few jumping jacks to get the blood pumping, and she was still going. "Oh, and mention the possibility of doing a blue-pink, green-yellow swirl if she likes that idea better. The bakery said they could do that too."

"Good night, Josie." I yawned before firing up Old Bessie, successfully ending the conversation with the cacophony of the truck's engine.

Before even touching the gas, I unscrewed the Thermos lid and took a sip of the coffee to make sure it wasn't scalding hot. If it was, I didn't seem to care, because I chugged half of the contents before settling it between my legs and rolling out of the driveway. Unlike the Sterling-Walkers' driveway, the Gibson-Blacks' was pocketed with rocks and pot holes. It didn't take me long to realize I shouldn't have settled an open Thermos of coffee between my legs. It might not have been scalding, but it still burned when it seeped through my jeans.

Instead of tightening the lid back into place, I downed what was left. The caffeine didn't seem to hit my system until I pulled up to Willow Springs. I'd barely been able to stay awake on the drive, so of course the caffeine would go into effect now that I was ready to crawl into bed.

Everything was quiet. The house was dark, not even a flicker of a computer glowing in one of my sisters' rooms. The barn was quiet. Even the night was quiet. When I checked the time on my phone, I saw that if I fell asleep the moment my head hit the pillow—which was unlikely —I'd get a solid five hours of sleep before I had to be up to help Dad and the rest of the hands with the cattle. Just thinking about it made me more tired—forget the caffeine charging through my system.

Stumbling up the porch stairs, I forced myself through the front door and only realized I'd forgotten to close it when I was halfway down the hall. Getting back to the open door felt like a journey, but after getting it shut, locked, and double-checked just to make sure my eyes weren't playing tricks on me, I shuffled into the living room. I wasn't sure if she would be awake, but if she wasn't, I'd crash on the couch. I didn't want to wake her by sliding in beside her. She needed her sleep more than I did.

I'd barely stepped into the living room when her head whipped in my direction. Even from here and even in my beat state, I noticed her eyes widen, followed by a sigh that was brimming with relief.

"You shouldn't have driven home like that," she said, waving at me as I staggered toward her. Her voice was stern, but she couldn't hide her smile. She was happy I was there, glad I'd made it home for the night. I was even more so. "Getting behind the wheel in your condition is worse than drowning yourself in whiskey and driving. I need you alive, please."

I grinned as I finished my journey toward her. I felt drunk. But the happy kind of drunk. The warm, tingly kind. Rowen did that to me. She made me feel all warm and happy and tingly.

Kicking off my boots, which was more like almost tripping over them, I crawled in beside her—she'd already scooted over to make room—roped my arms around her, and lowered my head on the pillow beside hers. I was home.

"I need you alive too, please."

CHAPTER ten

Rowen

HE WAS GONE. I didn't have to open my eyes to know it. I could practically feel the side of the bed he slept on was cold and empty. I didn't like waking up after he'd slipped away without me noticing. I knew why he didn't wake me before leaving—he was obsessed with me getting every wink of sleep I could—but I didn't like starting my day without him. It just didn't feel right. Like it was a bad omen.

Most mornings I stirred before he'd fully rolled out of bed at four. It was our chance to have a few quiet minutes alone to share a cup of coffee and pretend life was as easy and breezy as it wasn't. I hadn't missed a morning with him in a few weeks, so that was probably why I was feeling extra-strength grumpy when Lily came into the living room at nine in the morning. As was her routine, she knocked on the wall just outside, like it was a door and she was announcing herself, and waited for an invitation to come in. I found it especially endearing.

"Enter if you dare," I called, smoothing my hair and blankets so I didn't look like a banshee and frighten the girl. I woke up looking more like a wild animal than a woman most mornings. Especially so since the bed rest.

"I dare." She stepped inside wearing a smile that implied she knew a secret no one else in the whole world was privy to. I loved those kinds of smiles. They were a side effect of love in its infancy, when you're certain no one else could ever know how you feel.

"What are you up to this fine morning?" I asked. Outside, the day was turning out to be a beautiful last-days-of-summer-meets-first-days-of-fall kind of day. If an eighteen-year-old girl didn't have big plans for a day like this, the world was doomed.

"Colt's coming to pick me up in a little while, but my chores are done, I can't mess with my hair for another moment, and was wondering if you'd like to kill a little time with me?"

Lily was wearing one of her linen summer dresses but had slid into a denim jacket to fight off the chill these kinds of mornings brought in. She was in a pair of shortie cowgirl boots and was wearing her hair down and swept over one shoulder. Unconsciously, I'd always pictured Lily as a girl. I'd never looked far enough ahead to see her as the woman she'd become, the one standing in front of me today.

If a sister-in-law could seem to just grow up overnight, how much faster would it seem my own child would? The thought made me mourn a day that was years and years away, almost making me wish the baby would stay in my stomach a little longer than expected.

That wish vanished in the two seconds it took for me to shift myself around in bed and feel like I was more a walrus with no arms or legs to assist me, just some giant thing trying to scoot along through life.

"I've got so much time to kill these days, it's not even funny." I eyed the chair beside my bed. Jesse usually used it to pull on his boots or drink his coffee in while we talked for a few minutes in the morning before he rushed out the door to spend a twelve- to fifteen-hour day working. "So please, come kill some with me together. Much more enjoyable that way."

She practically skipped across the room before floating into the chair beside me. Her smile would not be tamed. I doubted little could steal it from her.

"Someone's looking rather joyous this morning," I said, arching a knowing eyebrow. "This wouldn't have anything to do with getting to spend the day with your young beau, would it?"

Her eyes lightened a shade. "It would." She checked out the window.

I couldn't even begin to guess how many times I'd checked out that window for Jesse to come pulling up the driveway. No joke that a million was a closer estimate than a thousand.

"But we're only spending the morning together, not the whole day," she said. "I've got a bunch of things I promised Mom I'd help her with, and he's got to catch a flight back to California later this afternoon." Her boyfriend flying away was one of the few things that could wear at her smile.

"How long will he be gone?" I reached for the insulated cup of coffee Jesse had left for me and took a sip. It was decaf, but it still tasted good.

"A week this time. Only a week." From her tone, it was like she was trying to reassure herself.

"That's hard, isn't it? Managing a long distance relationship. Especially when you guys haven't been together very long."

Lily nodded and exhaled. "It's so much harder than I thought it would be. I don't know how you and Jesse managed it, especially with you guys only having been together a couple of months before you left for Seattle."

I lifted my shoulders. "We loved each other."

Lily smiled into her lap. "I know the feeling."

"This thing with him flying back and forth won't stop anytime soon, right?"

She shook her head, looking almost solemn.

"It might only get worse if he expands?" I said gently.

Her answer was a sigh. Colt had opened up a hip kind of barbershop in California, and it had been so successful, he'd added a second shop a half hour up the coast. Like the first, it had also done well, and I'd heard rumor that he was planning to add a few more in the next year. Of course Garth and Jesse's commentary didn't end for a solid week when they found out about pretty boy Colt Mason opening up a posh barbershop in southern California—it was like the best kind of irony for them. The jokes were still coming, although the original ones had gotten old. The newest ones circled around Colt expanding into tanning salons.

I respected Colt for wanting to make it on his own and not rely on his dad's money and name as his other brothers seemed content to do. Sure, the barbershop thing was kind of hilarious given how pristine Colt's hair always was, but hey, he knew hair and was clearly passionate about it. I say the more power to him. "So what are you going to do if he has to, like, officially move back to California to run his barbershop empire?"

Lily's gaze cut in my direction.

"I wasn't making fun. Promise. Totally serious."

She'd taken enough crap from her brother and brother's best friend to be a little sensitive about the word barbershop. "I'm going to cry. A lot." She wrung her hands in her lap. "And then I'll get on with life because what else can we do?"

"We can pack our bags and fly out to join the man we love for a long weekend."

"Yeah, I'm sure my parents and Jesse would just love that. They'd probably require I have my own room on an opposite wing of the house, and they'd fit me with one of those cameras on top of my head so they could monitor every little thing said and done."

I patted her knee. Romantic life was rough for the oldest daughter of an old-fashioned rancher. "Good thing your facial structure would really complement a camera wrapped around your forehead."

She laughed with me for a moment, then it looked like she was about to cry.

"Lily?" I squeezed her knee.

She ran her fingers through her hair. "You can't choose who you fall in love with, you know? If you could, Colt Mason would have been at the bottom of my list. My brother hates him, along with just about all of my other guy friends—"

"Jesse doesn't hate him," I interrupted. "He just doesn't like the idea of him being your boyfriend. Not that he'd like the idea of any other guy being your boyfriend any better . . . and your guy friends don't like him because they wish they'd have worked up the courage to ask you out before Colt did."

She gave a small huff. "Well, of course. Who

wouldn't want to go out with me?"

"The only guy who wouldn't want to go out with you is the kind who likes his girls as vapid as he likes them shallow."

Lily shifted, as expected. Compliments were like enduring torture for her. "So put Jesse and my friends aside, but there are only a half million more reasons Colt and I shouldn't be together."

"Like what?" It was my turn to shift when Baby Sterling-Walker decided to give me a solid kick to the belly button. He was getting strong. So strong, some kicks felt as if they were close to popping right through my skin.

"Like that he's older than me."

"Seems like a big deal now, won't even matter in another five years."

"He comes from a rich family who made their fortune making movies, not working the land, which is kind of sacrilegious out here."

I shook my head. "They earned their money working hard, just like everyone else out here has. Don't let the details muddy the waters."

"People think he's conceited and too good for me and is only into me because he wants to be the one to . . . you know . . ." If I didn't know before, her reddening face filled in the dot, dot, dot.

"Here's my mantra, Lily. One of them at least. Hold it close." I rolled onto my side so I could look at her straight on. "People suck. Big time and most of the time. Who gives a crap what a bunch of people are saying? People are going to talk, and they're going to talk shit. Don't let a bunch of shit talkers keep you from doing what you want and loving the people you want."

Lily watched me for a moment. Then she blinked. "People suck," she said slowly, as if she were tasting the words, testing them.

"You just think that, say that, or scream that the next time you start to let people's opinions on you and Colt get to you, okay?"

Her smile crept up on one side. "I think I can do that."

"Good." I fired off a wink and took another drink of my coffee. "You can't choose who you fall in love with, that's true. If we did, I'd probably be on some roller coaster of a relationship with some emo rocker guy who wears eyeliner and reads dark poetry but doesn't understand a lick of it and has a time limit of two minutes when it comes to making love."

Lily laughed, and I couldn't help laughing too. I'd dated a string of those types of guys before marrying a wholesome cowboy from Montana. Destiny's a funny thing.

"Speaking of people you can't choose in your life . . ." Lily bit the corner of her lip. "Mothers fall into that category too."

My eyebrows pinched together. I thought she was talking about Rose, who was the dream when it came to moms of teenage girls. Only a few moments later, I realized it wasn't her mom she was talking about. It was mine.

"I'm not disagreeing, but I'm curious where you're taking this," I said, feeling the hairs on my arms rise from just thinking about the mother I hadn't seen since that summer when she'd brought that scum of a guy back into her and my life.

"I'm just saying that I'm here if you ever need to talk about it, you know?" she said, picking each word carefully. "It's got to be hard being pregnant, about to become a mom yourself, and not have any contact with yours."

"It would be harder if I did have contact with her, trust me."

Lily nodded, back to staring at her lap. "Have you been able to get in touch with any of your other family? You know, to invite them to the baby shower if you want?"

I swallowed. "There isn't any other family, not in the sense I've learned from you all what family really is." Damn hormones were making my eyes burn with tears I could feel just waiting to be released. "I've got my family. Right here. The others might share the same kind of blood as me, but they wouldn't bleed for me the way this family would. The way I'd bleed for this family."

She took my hand and shared a smile. "So you won't be upset if your blood family isn't at the shower? Or part of your baby's life?"

"Not in the least. I want my baby to learn what family should be, not what they shouldn't. He can learn that from all of you Walkers. You guys sure made a believer out of this skeptic." I wiped at my eyes to show those forming tears who was in control, but one snuck past me.

That was when we heard the telltale sound of tires crunching over gravel. Colt's truck sounded more like Garth's beefy diesel than Jesse's, but they both made the same amount of noise rumbling up the driveway.

"Your coach awaits." I gave a grand flourish of my arm at the window Lily was already smiling through.

"Do you want me to grab you anything before I leave?" She rose out of the chair and waved out the window when Colt's truck rolled to a stop outside.

"I'm good. Thanks though." I waved at my easel beside my bed, prepped and ready with a blank canvas. My morning was off to a brighter start from thinking of what I'd create that day.

"If you need anything, give me or Colt a ring. I think Mom and my sisters are at the library in town, and Dad and Jesse might be out in no-reception land."

"And by no-reception land, you mean they could be just about anywhere on the ranch?" I said.

She chuckled with a nod. "Isn't Montana great?"

"The best. Hey, have fun," I called as she moved out of the living room with a wave. "And remember, people suck."

"People suck." The words came out a bit more natural sounding, almost as though she might be able to convince herself of it the next time she heard a nasty rumor circling around her and Colt.

After the door slammed shut behind her, Colt's truck rested in the driveway long enough that I could guess what they were doing. Especially with all of the parental figures and overprotective older brothers out of seeing and hearing range. I couldn't help smiling. Lily was happy. With Colt Mason. I might not have ever considered the possibility, but that was what made it so wonderful. The thrill of the unexpected. The reminder that just when we think we might be starting to figure life out, it went and surprised the hell out of us.

A few minutes later, Colt's truck pulled out of the driveway, and I got to work getting my supplies and canvas ready to go. I'd learned yesterday, through trial and error, that positioning was everything. If I had too many blankets or pillows stacked around me, it inhibited me. If I had too few, I got weird aches and pains in my back and neck. If the table holding the easel was too far away, my arm started to shake after five minutes. If it was too close, it cramped. Two months on bed rest, and I'd lost whatever semblance of strength I'd possessed. I would probably get winded taking the baby out for a walk after all of this.

Today I was planning on working with charcoal, and I'd just made my first few sweeps across the canvas when the charcoal fell from my hand. My body froze at the same moment I felt a chill crawl down my spine. My breath caught for what felt like a long moment, then, as if someone had just pressed a pin into my frozen balloon, everything turned to chaos within me.

My breath restarted, but it found an erratic pace and couldn't be calmed. My heart matched my lungs' crazed pace. Before I knew what I was doing or rationalized that I shouldn't have been doing it, I shoved the table with the easel away and leapt out of bed. As was typical every morning I got out of bed for the first trip to the bathroom, I felt a wave of dizziness, but I didn't give myself a moment for it to clear before I lunged forward.

Instinct took over. As my feet rushed for the front door, I at least found the sense to grab one of Jesse's big canvas coats. I was in my standard bed rest wear, and a tank top and cotton shorts weren't the best things to be rushing around outside in, especially when I was still braless.

As soon as I was out the door, I paused, reason catching up with me. What was I doing? Why was I out there? What had hit me so violently and suddenly, it was like my subconscious had just been smashed into by a semi?

I cleared my head for a second and calmed my breathing for that same moment, but it was enough. A sound. I'd heard a sound. A loud one. An unnatural one. That sound had been followed by a feeling as jarring and violent as the sound.

Looking around at what was close by, I couldn't see anything, and I didn't know where the sound had come from, but I started down the dirt road leading in the direction of where I knew they'd recently moved the cattle. Part of me felt crazy for rushing down a bumpy, grassy road when I was supposed to be on bed rest, but the other part of me couldn't be coaxed back. Reason and instinct were battling it out, but instinct was winning. I kept going, holding my stomach and trying to keep my heart and breath from getting away from me.

I might have had the sense to slip into a coat to ward off the morning chill, but I'd forgotten all about shoes. With every step, more mud and dirt lodged between my toes and spackled up my calves. The earth was cool, cold almost, and it sent a chill up the pads of my feet that seeped into the rest of my body.

I kept pushing forward, fighting the name going through my head and what had happened to ignite this primal feeling. I shoved the what ifs aside and kept running, convincing myself that I didn't know exactly what I was rushing to or what I'd find when I got there, but also knowing who I'd find and what I'd find.

It was a gut feeling. I knew it with absolute certainty, though I had no way to explain it or go about proving it if I was asked to. The farther I ran, the more I wished I had grabbed a set of keys for the ranch trucks. I was eight months pregnant—eight months pregnant and on indefinite bed rest. I shouldn't have been sprinting down some back road, feeling one lunge away from tripping over my own feet as I charged forward.

That gut feeling rolled to a boil in my stomach and came to an explosive burst when I reached the crest of the small hill I'd just tore up. My stomach leapt into my throat, my throat into my mouth, and I came to a screeching stop. I teetered in place, the sound of my hurried breath echoing in my ears.

My knees felt like they were about to give out and my legs were screaming from the exertion, but I forced myself to keep moving. I made myself take another step, then another, until I was back to sprinting. But this time I knew exactly where I was sprinting.

Old Bessie was off the side of the rudimentary road, the front half of her wrapped around a tree.

I choked on a sob, knowing who'd been behind the wheel. I choked on another when I found myself wishing it was someone else, anyone else, who'd asked to borrow Jesse's truck to make a quick run.

With the road being so rough, a driver couldn't go much faster than twenty-five down it, but from the direction Jesse had been coming before hitting the tree, I guessed what had happened to make Old Bessie look as though the tree had crushed her entire front half: Jesse had fallen asleep at the wheel, and the truck had picked up speed coming down that hill. Enough speed to cause that kind of collision.

It couldn't have been more than a quarter of a mile from the top of the hill where I'd first seen the wreck to actually getting to Old Bessie, and I was running as fast as my short legs would take me, but I felt like something had gotten its claws into me and was holding me back from where I was desperate to get.

"Jesse." Why was my voice a whisper? I was trying to scream. I needed to scream. I needed to get someone's attention and get some help. "Jesse." Another sob burst up my throat when my word came out so softly, I could barely hear it.

I tried again, but nothing came out that time. No words were possible, because I'd finally gotten close enough to see him. He'd been driving, just as I'd known. His head was angled away from me, his arms and chest wrapped around the steering wheel like he was giving it a hug. His hat was missing, and there was a round fracture in the windshield where I guessed his head had hit on impact.

My feet finally got away from me. When I was a few steps away, I tripped and went sprawling to the ground. I managed to get my arms around in front of me to break my fall enough that my knees took the brunt of it instead of my stomach. I felt the cool mud caking my knees and shins, and at the same time, I noticed a robin in the tree above me. The tree Jesse had crashed into. The bird was chirping, singing a song, carrying on with its life as if life was still going on. But it wasn't. It couldn't be.

Planting my hands into the dirt, I pushed myself up, using the door handle to help. "Jesse." I wasn't sure if I'd managed to verbalize it that time or not, but his name echoed in my head.

The driver's side window was rolled down, so I reached in to settle my hand on his shoulder. I gently shook it. He didn't move. I ran my hand over to his other shoulder and gave him another shake. Harder this time. He still didn't move. When I pulled my hand back, I found it painted red. It wasn't the kind of color I was used to streaking my hands. It didn't look the same or even feel the same. It was warm. Sticky. It made my stomach roil.

His name slipped from my lips as I tried to wipe his blood coating my hand off on the coat. I couldn't. It wouldn't all come off. It had worked its way into the lines and creases of my palm and would not be rubbed away.

"Jesse." I stopped wiping at my hand and ran around to the passenger side. I threw the door open, crawled inside, and slid across the bench seat toward him. "Oh my god, Jesse. Don't do this. Not now. You were supposed to be the one our baby had as a guarantee. I was the one who was supposed to go if one of us had to. Not you."

I draped myself around him, almost like he was draped around the steering wheel, a string of silent prayers on my lips. I was in my own world, stuck in it with the man I loved and the one it seemed like I'd have to spend the rest of my life without.

That might have been why I didn't really hear the truck rush up behind us or hear the doors being thrown open or the voices crying our names. I didn't really hear anything until someone's arms wrapped around me and tried to pull me back. Then I fought. I didn't want to be pulled away. I wanted to stay right there with him. I didn't want to be separated from Jesse.

"Rowen?" a familiar voice cried behind me. "What are you doing here? Oh my God. Is he okay, Colt? Is my brother okay?"

I continued to fight against Colt's strong grip, but he pulled me out of the truck and handed me off to Lily before crawling back into the truck, his cell phone to his ear. I struggled against Lily at first, but it didn't last. My fight gave out a few squirms later, and all that was left were my tears. I dropped to my knees, and Lily fell to the ground beside me. She wasn't crying though. Her face was white with shock, her eyes so wide they seemed to take up her whole face as she went from staring at her brother trapped inside the car to the front end of the truck buried against that giant tree.

"I need to report an emergency," Colt said into the phone, his fingers pressed to Jesse's neck.

Oh, God. He was checking for a pulse. Why hadn't I thought of that? How had I known? Why had I run what had to be close to a mile when I wasn't supposed to walk up a flight of stairs? Why were Lily and Colt here? What would happen?

So many questions spilled through my mind, piling up one upon the next. Then the one I wanted to hide from more than all of the others: was he alive?

I didn't want to ask Colt what his fingers felt, pressed into the side of Jesse's neck. I didn't want the answer, because part of me knew that Jesse didn't look like his eyes would ever open up again. Those eyes that could express so much with so little effort might never see the face of the child we'd made together. He might never feel what it was like to cradle a firstborn for the first time in his arms. He might never hear the first hiccup or coo or cry our baby would make.

As Colt talked to the operator, I wept. I wept for what might have been and what had been. For would could be and what might never be. I wept until my breaths turned into gasping sobs while beside me, Lily remained a pale statue. Colt was the only one with a semblance of calm.

Colt was still on the phone, giving what sounded like directions, when I crawled back toward the truck. Back toward my husband. I needed to be near him. Lily didn't hold me back this time. All she could do was stare inside the cab of Old Bessie and shudder. My crawl came to an abrupt stop when something ripped down my stomach. I couldn't help the howl that rushed out of my mouth. Wrapping my arms around my stomach, I rocked onto my side, totally bowled over from the pain. I lifted my hand to my face, sure I'd find it coated in blood again. My stomach felt as if it had been torn open.

There was no blood, but when the next jolt of pain came, I knew what was happening. I'd felt it weeks ago, though nothing to this degree. It was the whole reason I'd been put on bed rest. The whole reason I'd been confined to a bed for two months.

To keep my body from going back into labor.

Too late. They might have been able to stop it the first time, but something about this whole doomed day told me there'd be no stopping my labor a second time. The baby was coming.

When the third contraction hit me, I cried louder, but it was less due to the pain and more to the thought that the very day our baby would be born was the same day it lost its father and I lost my husband. A new love of my life was entering the world, and another was leaving it.

"Lily," I panted, trying to sit up to get her attention. I could barely move. "Lily." When I tried a third time, it came out as a scream thanks to the contraction tearing my body down the middle. "Lily!"

Her eyes cleared before they moved to me, spread out on the ground in front of her. They went wide again when she noticed the way I was breathing and holding my stomach.

"The baby," I breathed. "It's coming."

Her eyes went wider for one second, then a look of resolution fell over her face before she scooted toward me and placed my head gently in her lap. "Colt!"

He stopped mid-word.

"Tell them to send another ambulance." When his brows pinched together, Lily sucked in a deep breath. "Rowen's in labor."

CHAPTER eleven

Rowen

THE AMBULANCE TOOK me first. It took me instead of him.

The second one had arrived as they were loading me, so it wasn't like more than a few minutes had passed since the time the first one arrived, but they'd taken me first. Why? Was it a simple case of there being two lives endangered with me—mine and the baby's—or did something else go into the prioritization of rescue victims? Something having to do with who they could save versus who was past the point of saving?

Lily leapt into the ambulance with me, leaving Colt with Jesse. She kept shushing me and running her fingers through my hair as I fired off questions, demanding the medics tell me why they'd picked me and not my husband. No one gave me an answer, so I was left with my guesses.

I hated leaving Jesse like that. I hated being unable to do anything about it too. When he needed me most, I'd left him. Colt stayed and promised me he'd ride in the ambulance with him and call the Walkers, but I didn't miss the way Colt couldn't seem to look me in the eyes when he talked to me. I didn't miss the streaks on his shirt, painted red with the blood of my husband.

The drive to the hospital was surprisingly fast. I supposed that was what a set of blaring sirens and trained drivers would do, but once I was rolled through the emergency room doors, I went one-track minded. The quickening contractions were the only thing that could distract me from firing off question after question to whatever hospital employee was close enough to hear me. I wanted to know if Jesse had arrived yet. If so, where had he been sent? Could we be placed in rooms next to each other? Could they please go and check on his status? Could they let him know our baby was about to be born and I really wanted to wait until he was awake and nearby to witness it?

Whenever I got back around to that last question, I crumbled around another bout of sobs, knowing that even if he did make it, he wouldn't make it to the birth of our child.

Lily stayed with me the entire time—they let her too. When they got me settled in a room and started hooking me up to every last machine and monitor in the place, I blurred everything out. I had to. None of this was going the way I'd planned, hoped, or even guessed it would. Yes, I knew my pregnancy was high risk, but I'd never thought that would translate to delivering weeks early after sprinting a mile, when I was supposed to be on bed rest, to discover my husband had wrapped his truck around one of the old trees on Willow Springs. A tree that had seemed so beautiful had become a device of death.

Lots of shouting and brash words were thrown around in my room, but I didn't pay attention long enough to catch what was being said. Between thinking about Jesse and trying to keep from vomiting from one contraction to the next, those efforts took up all of my energy.

When the contractions felt like they were on top of each other—the fall of one easing into the peak of another—my tireless questions ended. I couldn't even manage a word cursed in pain, so countless questions hollered down halls were out of the question. I wasn't sure how my heart was managing it or how much longer it would, but in the midst of the fear I was losing Jesse, it felt like some invisible strength of will branched out from deep inside of me and gripped on to the baby for dear life. I wouldn't lose them both. I wouldn't allow it.

For the moment, my heart seemed to be cooperating with me. For once.

Through it all, Lily stood beside me, holding my hand and standing tall. Every once in a while, when I glanced over, I'd find her skin had that same pallor and would feel her hand tremble in mine, but she didn't leave. She never eyed the door like she wanted to leave. She stayed beside me, in the middle of no doubt worrying about her brother like I was.

One of the nurses had been yelling at me to push for a while, but I continued to answer her with a shake of my head. I was still holding on to some sliver of hope that Jesse would come rolling into the room, in a wheelchair with a few bandages and maybe a cast or two, and make it for the birth. It was a fool's hope, but right then, I was the very epitome of a fool. If being a fool meant holding onto the hope that he was alive, then make me a fool forever.

The nurse looked close to being about to beg me or threaten me when someone rushed inside the room. It wasn't the someone I'd hoped for, but Josie brought with her a tender smile and a warm hand to hold. Sweat was pouring from my face, mixing with my tears, and my body felt as if it were about to explode, but when she brought a cold washcloth to my forehead and gave me a nod, it brought me back to a place of reason.

"Come on," she said. "Let's get your baby taken care of, and then we'll deal with the rest." She squeezed the washcloth, and icy cold droplets dripped onto my forehead, seeming to clear the crazed fever I'd been overtaken with. "Your baby needs you right now. Jesse's in good hands, and Garth's in there to make sure of it too. It's time to do your thing."

"But Jesse . . ." I bit my lip as another contraction ripped through my body. "I wanted him to be here. He wanted to be here."

Josie tipped her head, thinking for a moment, before pulling out her phone. "Do you want me to, you know, film it? So he can watch it later if—"

Her voice cut off abruptly, but I didn't miss her meaning. *If* he woke up. *If* he survived. *If* our baby would have its father. I shook my head, though it was for a different reason than the one Josie assumed.

"Yeah, good idea. It looks like a massacre down there. I'm not sure I could hold the camera steady." She smiled at me and gave my hand a hard squeeze. "Now listen to the 'pushy' nurse and push that baby out already."

I knew she was right. I knew I didn't have a choice. Or I did, maybe, but it was my job to take care of our baby. I had to trust that the doctors were doing theirs and taking care of Jesse. Once the baby was delivered and safe, then I could worry about Jesse, but worrying about him right now wouldn't do anything but hinder the whole situation.

"I'm ready," I panted at the nurse. "My baby? It's early. Will it be okay?"

The cross nurse's face relaxed, and she gave my knee a gentle squeeze. "Your baby's going to be okay. Let's get it out so you can see for yourself though. Okay?"

I couldn't answer her because that was when another contraction assaulted me, and this time when she and the doctor yelled, "Push," I listened. It actually felt pretty good, or at least like I could control something instead of just lying there and taking the contractions. Pushing, in a way, felt like I was fighting back.

On my third or fourth push, things got uncomfortable again, and I could guess why. More from the look on Josie's face—which made it seem like she was watching an autopsy—than from what the doctor was saying about the baby's head crowning.

"Oh my God," Josie said, looking away one second only to look back the next. "It's the most amazing and grotesque thing I've ever witnessed." She shook her head. "How in the hell is that possible? The next time a guy says he's tough, I'm going to make him watch a video of this."

The pain was unreal at that point. So searing white-hot it blinded me and brought me to a place where I felt like I was about to pass out and actually hoped I would. I'd never really given natural delivery much thought because I'd known from the very beginning that I'd be having a scheduled Caesarean. I'd never spent any time researching or thinking about what this would feel like or what the pain would do to me. I knew there were things like epidurals or spinal blocks or something for women who went with the traditional way of delivering a baby, and damn, I wished that was an option for me. But my baby was minutes, if not seconds, from being brought into the world. I think they'd told me when I'd been rushed in that I was too far along for the Caesarean to be safely performed, but I hadn't realized what that meant until right now, when my body felt as if it were simultaneously on fire and about to implode. If I ever did this again, I was going Caesarean all the way, even if my heart wasn't a factor in the equation. No question.

When the doctor ordered me to push again, I was already bearing down, desperate to make pain end. Then, all at once, it did. A relieved exhale rushed out of my mouth as my head crashed back into the pillow. And that was when I heard it—the cry. Our baby's first precious, gut-wrenching cry. I held on to the sound of it, memorizing every note and nuance so I could describe it in perfect detail to Jesse.

The doctor stood and smiled at me. "Congratulations. You've got a daughter."

CHAPTER twelve

Rowen

JESSE HAD BEEN right. Our baby was a girl. I should have known.

I'd been so convinced that we were going to have a boy that when the doctor told me it was a girl, it didn't register at first. Only after Lily, then Josie, had repeated it, then I'd cycled it through my head a few times, did I realize the little boy I'd been dreaming about had been, in fact, a girl all along.

It brought on a fresh rush of tears, but these tears weren't spawned from pain but from joy. We had a daughter. She was here and healthy, and I'd made it through the delivery healthy as well, my heart staying strong.

I didn't get to hold her—with her being premature, they had to rush her off to the Neonatal Intensive Care Unit—but the nurse made sure I got a good look at her before they whisked her away. She was, by a large margin, the most beautiful thing I'd ever seen. All pink and new and strong-lunged. She didn't stop wailing from the time she'd been born to the time they rolled her out of the room, and I loved that. I adored that in her first moments on this planet, she was already raising a riot and making sure she was heard. I cherished the thought that maybe, just maybe, wherever Jesse was and whatever condition he was in, he might be able to hear the first cries of our daughter.

After I'd been stitched up and cleaned up, they moved me to a different room in the main part of the hospital. I still had to be hooked up to that dreaded heart rate monitor, but I was so tired after the delivery, I was dozing off before they even dialed down the volume on the monitor.

Josie and Lily moved with me to the new room, and it wasn't long after that before Hyacinth and Clementine found us. The girls came in with smiles, but their eyes were puffy and rimmed with red. It was that kind of day for us all. A day of celebration and tragedy. I didn't want to ask either of them if they knew what was happening with Jesse, so I whispered to Josie, pleading with her to go find out something. Now that the baby was safe, I needed to know what was happening to the rest of my family.

She agreed, but I didn't miss how she dragged her feet as she left my room. I guessed she felt the same way we all must have—that she was as terrified of finding out how Jesse was as she was anxious.

Lily and her sisters stayed with me, but I hadn't seen either Neil or Rose, which meant they were with Jesse. Eventually Lily shuffled over to the window, staring out of it like she was trying to make sense of the day. I waited.

I waited some more. When it felt like the waiting would kill me and I was tempted to holler at whatever nurse walked by the door, I waited some more. I checked the clock on the wall so many times that when Josie finally made her reappearance, I could confidently say I never wanted to see another wall clock.

When she came into the room, all of us girls sucked

in a deep breath. She was staring at the floor, her hands wringing in front of her. I stopped breathing. My heart stopped too.

Then a sharp sob fell from her lips before she lifted her head. Her eyes found mine and in them was all the answer I needed. "He's alive."

CHAPTER thirteen

Jesse

IT HAD NEVER felt so good to be alive.

Holding my little girl, swinging on the porch swing hanging from the roof of our finished home, hearing the rest of my family's voices and laughter coming from inside. Life had been good for a long time, but now? Now it was great.

I'd spent months crippled by fear that I'd lose one or both of them, and they'd both made it. Rowen and our baby had survived the whole terrifying process and were just as healthy as could be. I should have put a little more faith in Rowen's reassurances rather than letting fear take center stage for so long, but that was behind me. I was looking to the future.

My daughter caught sight of a deer bounding past the house, and she bounced in my lap, making excited coos and pumping her fists. She could sit on this swing, content to watch life and nature roll by, almost as long as I could. I'd been doing a lot more of that lately—sitting and finding solace in quiet moments and unhurried schedules. Coming face to face with one's maker and surviving to live another day—or decades hopefully—had a way of changing a person's perspective. Facing death had a way of making life richer, a way of squeezing even more purpose into one's life, a way of bringing more meaning and significance to simple moments and everyday details. At least for me it had.

After two weeks in the hospital—our premature daughter had been discharged a week before I was—I finally got to go home. I needed to be sent home with a wheelchair and had graduated to crutches a couple of weeks after that, but I didn't have to have it confirmed by the doctors and nurses that I was lucky to be alive. A crash like that . . . the odds were more stacked against a person surviving it than they were stacked in their favor.

I didn't remember the crash. I didn't remember anything except for getting in Old Bessie and starting back to check on Rowen, then waking up in a hospital bed feeling like my body was one giant bruise. I had no memory of the two days that passed in between. Garth told me that was probably a good thing.

Of course the reason I didn't remember the crash was because I'd fallen asleep at the wheel. Exhaustion had chosen that moment to stifle me into submission. If nothing else, it had gotten my attention and respect. I'd never let myself get worn so thin again. I had a family to take care of, a family who depended on me. I had too much at stake to ever risk letting myself get that way again.

So the house had taken a lot longer to finish than I'd planned. Part of that was due to it being complicated, if not downright risky, moving around a construction site while using crutches. The other part of the relaxed build schedule had to do with my new life lesson of not wearing myself down to an exhausted nub again. Plus, I had a brand-new daughter to enjoy and get to know and a healthy wife I owed a serious debt. In more ways than one.

Living out of my parents' living room for the past ten months had been a bit . . . complicated and had taken more than one creative solution, but I'd never heard a single complaint from anyone. Everyone seemed relieved that we were all still there, a family that had grown one instead of shrunk one or more. But when the day came to finally move into Rowen's and my place, we were both ready to haul boxes over before the sun had risen.

It had been awesome of my parents to let us stay for so long, but we were ready for our own place. Some of the rooms were still being finished—our room still needed to be painted, the kitchen floor had just gone in last weekend, we were short a dining room table, and the garage still wasn't insulated—but there was a roof over our heads and all appliances of a necessary nature had been installed.

The picture Rowen had been working on for months at our old condo had been one of the first things to find its permanent home above the fireplace in the family room. She'd painted a portrait of the two of us, saving a spot in the lower center of the giant canvas for our baby to be painted in once it was born. I didn't know how she could make a painting more real than an actual photo, but I supposed that was part of Rowen's gift: turning art into reality, making it attainable even for some hick who'd grown up on a ranch in Montana. There wasn't one time I'd looked at that painting without feeling something—something that went deep enough it penetrated my soul every time.

We'd been in the house for just two weeks, but it already felt like home. It already felt lived in and like we'd lived years' worth of memories inside it instead of mere days. It was a good house. The kind that wasn't so large a person couldn't hear their child's laughter from across the house, nor was it so small it felt like there wasn't enough room to grow into it. It was just right. The place where I started and ended the day with my family.

Another couple of deer scrambled by the house, weaving through the maze of trucks and cars parked out front, and the little bundle in my lap exploded with motion and sound again. Just when I'd thought she was almost asleep. This was her typical naptime, but there'd been too much excitement inside for her to go down in her crib, so I'd slipped her out to the front porch. It was much quieter out here, even with the rushing creek in the background and the noisy birds yelling at each from across the valley.

Today was a special day—a day that had been months in the making and had finally come to fruition.

The front door opened, and out stepped someone who knew exactly who she was looking for and where to find them. The stern expression she tried to hold vanished the moment our daughter bounced in my lap again, flapping her arms like she was trying her hardest to fly to her mama.

"You know, this might not be a typical baby shower, but since the baby in question is out of my tummy, she should be present at this lavish party one of her godmothers threw for her."

Our daughter stopped bouncing for a moment, twisting her head back to look at me with big blue eyes that were as expressive as her mama's.

"Busted," I whispered to her.

She grinned a toothy smile and flapped her arms, all right in the world once again.

"Come on then, scoot over and make room." Rowen was already squeezing in beside us. "I need a break from the games and balloons and pastel-wrapped presents and napkins."

I gave her a little more room so she wouldn't be smashed into the arm of the swing, but not so much she wasn't still smashed against me. "I thought this was supposed to be a baby shower, not a royal coronation and wedding combined."

She leaned her head against my chest to get eye level with the eight-month-old who simply couldn't contain herself now that she had both Mom and Dad's attention. Rowen brushed her nose back and forth across our little girl's nose, making her erupt in laughter.

"Whenever Josie is at the helm of the party-planning ship, to expect anything less than over-the-top is to fool oneself," Rowen said, waving at the giant balloon arch leading up the porch before flashing her wrist in front of me to show off her ornate pink rose corsage.

"Not that I've been to a baby shower before, but I think this one hits upon a lot of firsts." I draped an arm around Rowen and rocked my family back and forth in the swing my dad had made for us as a home-warming gift. "Putting aside the fact that the baby is eight months old, there are guys here, a five-course barbeque dinner is planned, the mayor is a guest, and there's a bubble machine on our front walkway." I lifted my chin at the machine blowing an endless stream of bubbles.

"Plus, the mom-to-be-slash-already-has-been-for-eight-months is drinking a beer." Rowen lifted her bottle and winked. It was the same kind I'd been drinking that night her attempts to get me drunk and take advantage of me failed. She'd been taking advantage of me plenty lately to make up for lost time, no beer required. "And I made a special request for the bubble machine, so that's the one thing Josie isn't to blame for. The rest you can pin on her all you want though."

My brows came together as I studied the machine sending bubbles out across the field. My wife didn't strike me as the bubble-machine type. "You wanted a bubble machine?"

"She loves bubbles. Since she's kind of the star of the party, she should have a say in it." Rowen grinned at her daughter, who was going a little cross-eyed trying to focus on a bubble coming at her. It popped right between her eyeballs, and she giggled like it was the grandest thing in the entire world.

"Nice *she* finally has a name, right?" I said.

Rowen's eyes lifted to the sky. "Well, it wasn't like I was just going to name our child when you were unconscious. What if you had woken up to find out you had a child named Winnipeg or Desdemona?"

"I would have loved her every bit as much as I do now."

"Well, I wasn't going to take a chance, and besides, it wasn't like she needed a name during her first week of life. It's not like we've scarred her permanently because we didn't give her a name the moment she ejected out of my—"

My grimace must have stopped her. Either that or her memory of the whole birth. From what Garth had told me from what Josie had told him, war documentaries portrayed less carnage.

I nudged her. "I'm glad you waited. I'm glad we figured it out together."

"You and I might be the only ones. The rest of our friends and family were about to mutiny if we didn't give her a name, I think." Rowen held out her hands, and almost immediately, our daughter went into them. "But in plenty of cultures, a baby doesn't get named for days, even years. We were just being multicultural."

"*Sure,* we were," I said.

"What? You think I could have come up with a name like Elodie on my own? That brilliance took the two of our heads coming together."

At the sound of her name, Elodie looked between us, like she was answering with a *yeah, what is it?* Her name hadn't come from flipping through a list of old family names or even because of its meaning or origin—it had been far more simple than that. It was the one name both of us had had on our list of names we'd drawn up at the hospital. For others, that might have seemed an impetuous way to name one's child. For us, it was just the right way.

"Besides, you were the one who was convinced I was wrong about having a son, so I figured you'd have a list of girl names to bring to the baby-naming table." Rowen's gaze moved from Elodie to me.

The look in her eyes stopped my breath. Ever since the accident, some of the looks she'd given me could bowl me over if I wasn't bracing for them. It was almost as if she was looking at someone she'd buried and later seen risen from the grave.

"I was also just a little preoccupied, looming at your bedside in between visiting the NICU, worried my husband, who had just become a father, was going to ditch us."

I tightened my arm around her shoulders. "I wasn't going anywhere. Someone upstairs just figured I'd better learn a tough lesson before I became a dad and exhaustion took on a whole new meaning." I kissed her temple when I noticed Rowen's eyes glazing over. They'd done a lot of that ever since the accident. "There was and is no way I'm ever leaving my girls. Ever."

Rowen looked away long enough to wipe her eyes. "Did you hear that, Elodie? We've got Daddy's word on it now. He's not going anywhere."

Elodie made a few spit bubbles to show her support.

"What we always fail to bring up when we talk about that day is the one member of our family who moved on to greener pastures," I said solemnly, covering my heart.

Rowen slugged me. "Old Bessie had been needing to move on to greener pastures since the Reagan administration."

I sighed. "I loved that truck."

"I don't think you're having much of an issue conjuring up the same emotion for your new truck." She stared at our new truck, gleaming in the driveway. "Traitor."

"I will always carry Old Bessie right here in my heart, but I've got to say, heated seats in the winter and a working air-conditioning system in the summer are really great features."

Her elbow nudged mine. "Yeah, I miss her too. She was a good truck, but she died protecting someone she loved. That's a noble way to go out if there ever was one."

"Agreed," I replied with a nod.

"That guy from the insurance company was adamant

that if you'd hit that tree at that speed in anything less than the tank Old Bessie was, you wouldn't have, well, you know . . ."

My jaw tightened. "I know."

With a sniff and shake of her head, Rowen bounced Elodie in her lap a few times before rising. "I think we've dodged the party long enough. Time to get back to the festivities." Rowen lifted her eyebrows at Elodie. "After all, the mayor's in there."

"Only because one of Montana's up-and-coming artists is the guest of honor at the baby shower," I added, taking one last swing before standing beside my girls.

She let out a huff. "Only because the local golden boy drove his truck into a two-hundred-year-old maple tree after falling asleep at the wheel from getting a total of ten hours of sleep in the past month the very same day his wife with a severe heart condition decided to have their firstborn child."

It wasn't word for word, and she might have taken creative liberties with certain words, but it was close to the local newspaper's article that had been printed the week after the accident. There had been no shortage of follow-up articles either. Not because Rowen or I gave a darn about talking to the newspaper about that day, but because in a small town, that kind of stuff was big news. Rowen was convinced the mayor was only there to gather additional intel to pass off to the newspaper for yet another sensationalized article. I didn't know. I liked giving people the benefit of the doubt, but if we woke up tomorrow to find a detailed description about the Baby Born in Tragedy's baby shower, I definitely wasn't voting for the mayor when her reelection came around.

We were almost to the front door when it burst open, and out stepped one not-so-happy-looking Josie Black. True to their style, Garth and Josie hadn't been able to resist getting hitched a couple months back at some little chapel in Vegas when they'd been in town for the weekend for one of his rodeos. It was very much what we all would have figured from them. Josie's mom had about murdered them when she found out, but everyone was mollified by their big wedding reception a month later.

"What are you three doing out here when the party's in there?" Josie waved at where we were standing to inside, where I guessed she was implying we should have been standing. "Everyone's asking where you guys are."

"Sorry, sorry. We're coming." Rowen carried Elodie through the front door, and I followed. "We just needed a breath of fresh air."

"A breath of fresh air takes two seconds, not twenty minutes." Josie crossed her arms and gave me a look, guessing I was the ringleader of our escape.

I lifted my hands. "Thanks for the clarification. Consider me fully stocked on breaths of fresh air for the rest of the day."

As we made our way back into the packed living room, which had spilled over into the dining room and kitchen, I couldn't help but smile as I studied the faces of old friends and new ones, family members I saw every day and ones I hadn't seen in years, acquaintances I could place and some I couldn't . . . all of these dozens of people here to celebrate our precious child. Sure, Josie might have gone overboard with the décor, menu, and guest list, and I might have needed to escape for a while to catch my breath, but I was thankful for each person in the house, showing their support for our new family.

As Rowen wove through the room, no fewer than ten different sets of arms reached out to take Elodie, but Rowen wasn't ready to give her up just yet. She was almost as greedy when it came to time with our daughter as I was. Finally Grandma won out, and Elodie seemed thrilled with the outcome. My sisters gathered close by, each of them fretting with the hem of Elodie's dress or the position of the tiny bow in her hair or fixing a sock starting to slide off. She had as many doting extended family members as she did immediate ones—my daughter would never lack for love in her life.

"Hey, not sure there's a rule book or anything for this, but I'm winging it." Garth shouldered up beside me and handed me a beer. "Pretty sure it must fall in the godfather's list of duties that he keep the dad good and buzzed at the baby shower."

It was the same kind of beer Rowen had, and the memory made me smile. I'd been such a wreck for half a year and for what? Everything had turned out just fine. All of that worry and anxiety and those sleepless nights . . . they'd turned me into a fool who'd driven his truck into a tree.

"Hey, I'm already buzzed. Thanks though." I handed the beer back to Garth.

"Buzzed? All I've seen you downing is that pink fruit punch with ice cream and rubber duckies floating on top. I helped Josie make that junk, and there's nothing in there that a man from Montana should be drinking at a baby shower."

I held out my arms and winked. "I'm buzzed on life."

Garth rolled his eyes. "Asshole."

"Hey, you're Elodie's godfather. No cussing at her baby shower."

Garth grimaced. "You're right, Jess. Shit, I really have a lot to learn, don't I?"

I shook my head. Cursing was such an involuntary function for Garth, kind of like breathing, that he didn't even realize he'd said it half the time.

I made sure Elodie was out of hearing range before clamping my hands on his shoulders. "Shit, you really do, Black."

After flicking his hat down over his eyes, I made my way over to where my mom was waving a rubber giraffe, which had been a gift from Hyacinth, in front of Elodie. She studied it for a moment before snatching it in her pudgy little hands and almost immediately putting its ear in her mouth.

"Hey, Mom?" I called as I hurried toward them. "She's got that in her mouth."

My mom and Rowen exchanged a look as Hyacinth lifted the box the giraffe had come from. "That's because it's a teething toy, Neurotic."

I read the label twice to make sure before letting myself look sheepish. "Never hurts to double-check."

Old habits died hard. I might have moved past hypervigilance to the tenth degree, but I was still hitting it to the first, if not second at times. Like when I found my eight-month-old baby girl sticking items of a questionable toxic versus non-toxic nature into her mouth.

"Do you really think her godmother-slash-aunt would let little Elodie get hurt or anywhere close to it on her watch?" Lily stuck her hand on her hip and lifted an eyebrow at me.

"Excuse me. *One* of her godmothers," Hyacinth inserted, nudging Lily, or shoving her, I wasn't sure.

"Yeah, Jesse, chill out. There're three of us godmother-aunts close by, so Elodie's in good hands." Clementine gave the giraffe a squeeze.

When Elodie discovered that in addition to it being a fantastic thing to chew on, the giraffe also made a sound, her eyes looked like they would burst from the excitement of it.

"And a grandma," Mom added.

"And godmother number four," Josie piped up as she shouldered between Lily and Hyacinth to get her Elodie time. "Although since I was there to help bring you into this world and will teach you all you ever need to know about boys, I feel that slash-aunt part should be added to my godmother title."

I cleared my throat. "You will absolutely not be teaching her anything about boys because as far as my daughter is concerned, there is no such thing as anything male-species related."

Josie waved me off like I was talking the language of crazy, but I was more serious than she could guess.

Colt shouldered up beside me, giving Lily a smile when she glanced back. "We still on for next Friday?"

"We're still on," I replied, reminding myself to brush the chip off of my shoulder when it came to Colt. It had gotten easier since the accident, and according to Rowen, I'd made some serious progress in the civilized department when it came to Colt, but it was still a work in progress. However, she said sometimes I almost bordered on warmth.

I still wasn't hot on the idea of Lily and him together,

but I was willing to accept the fact that he was a decent guy who was one of the top three people responsible for my family being here today, healthy and happy. If it hadn't been for Colt and Lily showing up and what Rowen had recounted to me of Colt's calm-under-fire attitude in the midst of an emergency situation . . . well, our story might not have ended as happily as it had.

In one large way, I owed Colt Mason a debt I'd never be able to repay, so when he asked me to go fishing or invited the three of us out to dinner with him and Lily, I usually said yes. Colt wanted to be a part of the family, I knew that, and if Lily one day wanted that too, then I would support her and welcome him to the family with open arms.

As Colt took Lily's hand and steered her over to the food table, I called, "Hey, Colt?" I waited for him to glance back. "No more worms, okay? We'll do it the old-fashioned way."

He'd come a long in the de-Californication department, but the past few times he'd shown up for fishing, he'd come with a couple of Styrofoam containers of worms. How I was raised, a person didn't disgrace a fish by catching it with live bait.

"The old-fashioned way?" Colt's forehead wrinkled. Beside him, Lily rolled her eyes, and he said, "You mean, like, catching them with our hands or something?"

I had to work really hard to suppress that smile. "I mean fly-fishing."

Colt rubbed the back of his neck. "I've never been fly-fishing. I'm guessing I'll need a special rod and stuff for it, right?"

"I'll teach you. And I've got an extra pole you can

use."

Lily smiled at me.

Colt's forehead ironed out as he nodded. "Yeah, sure, that sounds great. See you Friday then."

I watched them make their way to the food table, but neither seemed to be hungry. At least not for the food.

"My, aren't you turning into a giant softie." Rowen came up beside me, Elodie back in her arms. I supposed that despite all of the doting aunts and godmothers and Grandma and everyone in between, no one beat Mom.

"Look who's talking," I replied, eyeing Rowen and Elodie, both in close-to-matching white linen dresses, both riding the line between grinning and giggling. "I seem to remember the girl I first met having a special affection for ripped fishnets and a hardened sneer."

"Didn't stop you from falling in love with me, did it?" That challenging glimmer flashed through her eyes. That hadn't changed. I doubted it ever would. At least I hoped it wouldn't.

"Nothing could have stopped me from falling in love with you." I dropped my head so our eyes were level, then I pressed my mouth against hers.

Elodie thought she'd contribute to the whole thing by snagging my bottom lip and giving it a tug.

"Ouch," I said, laughing when she gave it another tug.

"Welcome to fatherhood, babe." Rowen tried to pry Elodie's hand, one finger at a time, from my lip. The kid had an iron grip though. "And you're still sure you'll be able to manage this while I'm recovering? You'll be the main one doing her baths, and changing her diapers, and lifting her in the middle of the night, and playing when she decides three in the morning is the ideal time for peekaboo. I won't be able to do much those first few weeks after . . ."

I slipped my fingers under her chin and tipped it up. "I'm positive. And I'll love every second of it."

"Let's see if you're singing the same tune when Elodie's had her second bout of explosive diarrhea and you're changing her into her third set of pajamas for the night."

"I'll still be singing that tune," I said, though my words were a bit slurred due to Elodie's unwillingness to release my lower lip.

"Are you worried?" Rowen slid closer, hooking her fingers through my belt.

"A little," I said, "but I know your particular heart surgery is incredibly safe compared to other kinds of heart surgeries and that having it will mean we'll have you in our lives longer."

Her face softened, as if my words were calming whatever fears she might have about her heart surgery next month.

"And I know that after everything you went through and still managed to deliver our little girl, without any kind of pain relief, while worrying about what was happening to me a few rooms away, you've got to have one of the strongest hearts ever created."

She planted another kiss on me, so Elodie's fist got half and my upper lip got the other half. "You're right. So right. My heart is a god among mere mortals. A queen among peons. A rock star among the masses. There's nothing to worry about. Everything will be okay."

I felt my throat tightening, but I fought it. I wouldn't let fear guide my life any longer. "Everything's going to be great."

Rowen let Elodie finish crawling into my arms, and Elodie's other hand almost instantly went to my ear. She pulled and twisted on that too. Rowen laughed, shaking her head as our daughter yanked on my lip and ear like she was having a grand time. Hearing Mom's laugh made Elodie laugh. Hearing both of their laughs made me do the same. If there was ever a man who'd been more content with his life, I dared him to prove it.

When Elodie let go of my face a few moments later, she stopped bouncing and shrieking out giggles. She went from buzzing with movement and sound to complete stillness. In that brief moment, she looked at me in such a familiar way, I could have been sharing a look with her mama. She could say it all with one look, with one connection of our eyes. I hoped that though she might not have the words to define it yet, she felt what I was relaying back to her. My firstborn. My daughter. The second love of my life. If I could find a way to tell her anything in that silent exchange, I wanted her to know that she was my heart. She was my soul. She was everything that resided in between.

It had been that way from the first moment I saw her, a tiny, pink-skinned sleeping bundle in Rowen's arms. The love I felt for a being I'd just seen was so powerful, it would have knocked me over if I hadn't already been laid out in a hospital bed. Falling in love with our daughter . . . it was instant, instinctual, like it was predestined. Like our lives had been tied in the most intimate of ways in another life. I didn't need to touch her or hold her; all it took was one look, and she had me.

She was very much her mama's daughter.

THE end

OTHER WORKS BY NICOLE:

CRASH, CLASH, and CRUSH (HarperCollins)

UP IN FLAMES (Simon & Schuster UK)

LOST & FOUND, NEAR & FAR,

FINDERS KEEPERS

THREE BROTHERS

HARD KNOX, DAMAGED GOODS

CROSSING STARS

GREAT EXPLOITATIONS

THE EDEN TRILOGY

THE PATRICK CHRONICLES

about THE AUTHOR

Thank you for reading LOSERS WEEPERS by NEW YORK TIMES and USATODAY bestselling author, Nicole Williams. If you haven't read the other books in the LOST & FOUND series, FINDERS KEEPERS is the prequel to LOSERS WEEPERS, and LOST & FOUND, then NEAR & FAR are Jesse and Rowen's story.

In related news. . .
Jesse and Rowen will have one last chapter in their story (if you couldn't have guessed from the way this book left off!)! Their third and final installment in the series, HEART & SOUL, is available for pre-order now on Amazon, Barnes & Noble, and Apple. It will be officially released in June 2015

Nicole loves to hear from her readers.
You can connect with her on:

Facebook: Nicole Williams (Official Author Page)
Twitter: nwilliamsbooks
Blog: nicoleawilliams.blogspot.com

Made in the USA
Monee, IL
28 July 2020